She  **ing a tissue** ... **le short work of her tears and Ty in one swipe.**

Lord, I believe You want me in Plymouth, and not just for Andrea's wedding. Why, exactly, I don't know. But You've got to help me, or I won't make it out of Chicago. She banged the steering wheel again. *Please. Please.*

A semi's deafening air horn nearly sent her through the roof of the cab.

She glared into her mi... ...ng driver behind her. "Oka...

She fough... ...o Drive. "You kr... ...o get going, You cou... ...tead of *him*."

Her old se... ...gned a not-so-polite gesture at he... ...tor. Instead, a skinny smile tugged at her lips. "You're right, as always, Lord."

She pressed the accelerator. "It's time I moved on."

RACHAEL PHILLIPS

is a freelance writer in Indiana. She is married with three children. She has authored a novel, biographies, and co-authored a women's reference guide and novella collections, all for Barbour Publishing. Visit her at www.rachaelwrites.com.

Books by Rachael Phillips

HEARTSONG PRESENTS

HP1005—*The Greatest Show on Earth*

The Return of Miss Blueberry

Rachael Phillips

Heartsong Presents

Much love to our children, Beth, Christy, and David,
who shared many of the twenty-eight Blueberry Festivals
we experienced while living in Plymouth.

Special thanks to the wonderful people of Plymouth,
our longtime hometown, who blessed us with their friendship
and parked cars with us at the Blueberry Festival.

Deep appreciation to my critique partners, Kim Peterson and Jaclyn Miller,
for their encouragement and tough-love edits.

A note from the Author:
*I love to hear from my readers! You may correspond with me
by writing:*

Rachael Phillips
Author Relations
P.O. Box 9048
Buffalo, NY 14240-9048

ISBN-13: 978-0-373-48636-6

THE RETURN OF MISS BLUEBERRY

This edition issued by special arrangement with Barbour Publishing, Inc., 1810 Barbour Drive, Uhrichsville, Ohio, U.S.A.

Chapter 1

When Callie Creighton opened her eyes that May morning, the thought of quitting her dream job hadn't occurred to her.

But at a later meeting with her boss, he casually decimated her plans to be in her friend Andrea's wedding.

She longed to spit out, "You're fired!" and toss him through his omnipotent twentieth-story window into the Chicago skyline—or Lake Michigan, since she'd heard he didn't like to swim.

Instead, Callie sucked in a breath and sanded the gritty words in her mouth to smoothness before she spoke. "Mr. Stonewell, I believe you approved my vacation dates four months ago."

He was scrawling his signature on correspondence as if she'd already left the room. "Did I?"

"You did." Forcing a charming smile felt harder than pushing toothpaste back into a tube.

He didn't raise his pale, bulgy eyes. "That was before we landed the Turpin account."

We? She was the one who had grabbed that advertising contract before their competitors had a clue. Did he consider wrecking vacation plans a reward?

Her boss pushed the letters aside and scrolled on his smartphone. "We'll need you to clean up details before we start their campaign mid-September. Sorry, but you'll have to stay in town Labor Day weekend to finish the project and take care of any glitches." He stuck the phone to his ear, leaned back in his black leather chair, and fixed a cordial smile on his lips. "Hello, Jim? Glen here. I wanted to share new ideas I think will bump up your sales during the holidays...."

Callie waited.

Still talking, he gradually swung his chair around to the side.

Mr. Stonewell hadn't exactly turned his back to her. But his unspoken dismissal felt that final.

Turning to leave, Callie caught the heel of one of her new cut-out pumps on the carpet and almost fell headlong, spoiling her dignified exit.

No problem. It wasn't like her boss noticed.

Her tiny apartment usually presented a refuge after a hectic day's work. Today, though, Callie felt like she'd come home to a pink cave.

When Ty nicknamed it that, she'd defended her space as if it were a friend. What did Ty, who only felt at home in a stainless steel world, know about color?

He teased her about living in a Barbie house. She found her apartment a welcome relief from the soulless neutrals of the business world, though she did calm her pink walls with soft gray furniture.

Their uneasiness in each other's homes had kept them from

moving in together, a fact for which she now thanked God. Some empty evenings, she still missed Ty's edgy smile and conversation. God had rescued her, though she hadn't wanted His help.

Her pink walls closed in on her tonight, reminding her of Pepto-Bismol. She plopped onto her loveseat, hot, sour bubbles seething in her stomach.

Lord, what am I going to do?

She and Andrea Taylor, best friends since Miss Pringle read them *Green Eggs and Ham* at the library's Wee Wiggler Story Hour, had pinky-promised at their thirteenth birthday party to be bridesmaids in each other's weddings. How could Callie tell her she couldn't come to Plymouth? That she had to stay in Chicago on the biggest day of her friend's life to "clean up final details"?

She reached for the glass of raspberry tea on the end table and, instead, picked up the hideously cute black-and-white ceramic pig Andrea sent her after last year's Blueberry Festival. She ran her fingers over the red and pink roses on its back, growing more homesick every second. How long had it been since she'd attended the Festival? She couldn't remember.

The pig's goofy grin always made her smile. It fit perfectly in her funky little living room. Nobody else would give her such a gift. Certainly not Ty.

Andrea had become her sister. Without the love and encouragement of Andrea and her parents, Callie would have been sucked down the same alcoholic black hole as her own mother and father.

She set the pig on the table and glanced at the shoes that almost sent her sprawling in Mr. Stonewell's office. Andrea definitely would approve—of the shoes, not the lack of coordination—especially since Callie bought them at 30 percent off. She grinned. The Taylors might be wealthy, but they went grocery shopping on triple coupons day, as Callie did.

She gulped tea, but doubted it would settle her belly burner. Did she remember to buy antacids on her last trip to the drugstore? Lately, soothing her stomach after work had become a daily ritual, along with dosing major gastric disturbances when her employment difficulties escalated.

When her last impossible project kept her working more than seventy hours a week.

When Ben, her coworker, with Mr. Stonewell's blessing, pressured her into business tactics that made her feel dirty.

When her friend Sarah was unjustly blamed for a mistake and fired.

When…when…when… Callie's mind compiled a list of erupting office volcanoes. She realized they occurred monthly, with ever-increasing daily activity rumbling under the surface.

She gazed at her shoes again. Maybe she was thinking negatively. After all, what could she expect from a promising job? Callie loved the stimulating work that paid for occasional splurges at City Soles, frequent trips to downtown theaters, and gourmet cheesecake afterward, along with this cute apartment in a relatively safe, upwardly mobile neighborhood. Who would have thought a trailer-court girl from Plymouth, Indiana, could have made it this far, this fast?

Made it? A cold, clear thought interrupted. Exactly what have I made? Money, yes. But have I made a difference in anyone's life?

Well, she'd made Ty crazy. Mr. Stonewell, too.

But a positive difference?

In Plymouth, she'd been all about making a difference in the lives of kids who lived several trailers down. She'd cared about her aunt and alcoholic uncle, and even her cousin Brandy, though she put Callie down and always grabbed the bigger half when they split a candy bar.

Did she still care about her only blood relatives? Hallmark wasn't a very good substitute for hugs.

Callie stretched her neck to ease the tightness and slipped off her shoes. She grabbed her briefcase and padded to her bedroom to change. She needed a run to chase away the tension. A run to Grant Park then along Lake Michigan. Its vast expanse of blue sparkles and fresh breezes would dispel her clouds and give her focus. Then a walk as the sun hid behind the skyscrapers, with the dazzles melting into a milky, glimmering sea. She'd slow her body, mind, and heart and ask God what He thought about the whole situation.

And listen.

Mr. Stonewell waved Callie into his office. He was fiddling with his phone again. She glanced around at the room's sleek, colorless decor. Would she ever view Chicago from his window again?

"Is there a problem with the Turpin account?"

"No. In fact, I'm ahead of schedule." She'd grown used to his lack of greeting. "I've put in extra hours since I talked with you two weeks ago, and things should be in good shape by summer's end. Before Labor Day." Callie straightened her back. "Since the Turpin account will be ready to present, I'm again requesting Labor Day weekend off, so I can be in a friend's wedding."

"Friend? Not family?"

The Taylors are *family.* But she answered, "Yes. A friend since we were children."

"No. This project is too important to leave unsupervised. You're in charge. Stay in charge." He turned back to his phone.

Surprised that smoke didn't steam from her nostrils, Callie offered a silent 911 prayer then took a deep breath. "Mr. Stonewell, if I cannot take my vacation as planned, I'm afraid I'll have to leave my position, effective one month from today."

He raised his phone to his ear. His mouth stretched into a big smile.

She stared, and then realized he was, of course, preparing for an important pitch. He hadn't heard a word of her resignation.

Sure enough, he began an extended conversation about soda sales. Mr. Stonewell's tones swelled, softened, swelled again. He sounded like a beverage evangelist.

Though Callie longed to leave, she didn't move. Eventually her boss's gaze landed on her. His nose wrinkled as if she were a buzzing fly. He tilted his head slightly toward the door, which translated to "get lost." But she continued to fix her gaze on his bookcase, as if its contents fascinated her.

Finally he hung up and glared at her.

"Ms. Creighton"—he ground her name between his teeth—"we finished our conversation ten minutes ago."

"I don't think so, sir." She lifted her chin. "I don't believe you heard me. I gave you my resignation, effective one month from today."

For the first time in several years, she held Mr. Stonewell's complete attention.

"Why, why, *why*?" Since she was driving the U-Haul alone, Callie could yell and pound the steering wheel like a bongo drum. "Why did I ever think I could do this?"

She'd assured Andrea and her parents, who'd invited her to stay gratis as long as she liked, that she could handle this trip from Chicago to Plymouth herself. Then she'd take the South Shore train back to Chicago to pick up her SUV.

Now, surrounded by unmoving walls of semitrailers on Interstate 94, she needed a miracle to change lanes. Not so unusual. But as she peered in the side mirror, tears fogged her already limited view. "I'm not driving a truck," she shouted. "I'm driving a *garage*!"

She dropped her head to the steering wheel and sobbed like a six-year-old who'd taken the wrong school bus.

The traffic jam gave her plenty of time to cry. At first, after resigning, she'd felt brave, principled, and daring. Gradually, though, the last day of her employment loomed like an execution date. Now she had no job. Few prospects, though she'd spent hours filling out online applications. Like an elephant, her outstanding school loan balance had squished into the truck's cab with her. Had she deluded herself into thinking it wouldn't follow her to Plymouth?

She picked up her ceramic pig from the passenger side and hugged it, resting her slimy cheek on its red and pink roses. Minutes slogged by. An hour. Already she missed her apartment. Grant Park and Lake Michigan. Her favorite cheesecake place. Her friends, though she hadn't grown close to anyone but Ty.

Ty? Close? She'd sent him an e-mail about her move, like everyone else in her contacts. He didn't reply, didn't even text a good-bye.

She *wouldn't* miss Ty. Grabbing a tissue from her bag, Callie made short work of her tears and Ty in one swipe.

Lord, I believe You want me in Plymouth, and not just for Andrea's wedding. Why, exactly, I don't know. But You've got to help me, or I won't make it out of Chicago. She banged the steering wheel again. *Please. Please.*

A semi's deafening air horn nearly sent her through the roof of the cab.

She glared into her mirror at the grinning driver behind her. "Okay, okay."

She returned the pig to its seat and fought to shift the automatic gear into Drive. "You know, God, if You wanted me to get going, You could have sent an angel instead of *him*."

Her old self would have signed a not-so-polite gesture at her tormentor. Instead, a skinny smile tugged at her lips. "You're right, as always, Lord."

She pressed the accelerator. "It's time I moved on."

* * *

"Welcome to the Plymouth Walmart." Before the greeter could echo her words, Andrea yanked a cart loose from the stacked line and bowed grandly before Callie.

"Thank you, thank you." Pushing the cart, Callie acknowledged her friend's adulation with a celebrity smile and wave. "I can't tell you how long I've waited for this moment."

Trundling the aisles, both giggled like teens.

"I'm the one who's waited a long time," Andrea said. "I was beginning to think you'd never come home."

"I didn't intend to." Callie grabbed cables and a printer cartridge from a display. She needed to set up her computer. Without her company phone, she felt naked. Her laptop was on the fritz, and she hated to monopolize the Taylors' desktop.

She scanned the shelves, the displays, the faces of other shoppers who let them continue when their carts met in Saturday morning face-offs. The I-94 angst that nearly sent her back to Chicago on moving day had faded to nothing. "I've shopped in a gazillion Walmarts. Why does this one feel so much better?"

"Because you're with me." Andrea turned the cart to Health and Beauty. "That's the way it's supposed to be."

Even the fluorescent lights looked warmer here because she and Andrea were together. Because Plymouth was home... though she and her moving truck had chugged into Andrea's driveway only a few days before.

Callie had forgotten how a shopping trip to "pick up a few things" could grow into a major social event. They chatted with Andrea's coworker at the bank. Then with the elderly aunt of Patrick, Andrea's fiancé. Last, but not least, with Sam Whitaker, the pastor at Eastside Community, the church where they'd both grown up.

"Andrea told me a new pastor came to Eastside." Callie liked the fortyish man's invitation to call him by his first name and the faint smile wrinkles that revealed an optimistic outlook.

"Not so new." Sam's hazel eyes twinkled. "I've been here a few years now."

She couldn't picture anyone serving her old church other than Reverend Dansky, their childhood pastor. She'd have to remind herself that Plymouth wasn't a planet where everything stayed the same. Afterward, as they cruised to the checkout counters, Callie said, "Sam seems like a great guy."

"He's a special pastor." Andrea threw a package of batteries into the cart. "He'd just arrived in Plymouth when he helped me deal with Grandma's death."

A quiver invaded her friend's voice. Callie slipped her arm around her shoulders. Sometimes Andrea's sky-high confidence dwarfed Callie so that she almost forgot she towered over the petite woman. She hadn't seen this side of Andrea in a long time.

"I'm glad you're here again."

Callie barely heard the quiet words, but they stabbed her. What had forced her to leave immediately after the funeral? She couldn't remember. "I'm glad I'm here, too."

Andrea gave her a quick, hard hug, and then shoved the cart forward, as if her mission in life were to conquer Walmart.

After a chat with another of Andrea's friends by the card display, Callie said, "I'd forgotten how everybody knows everybody."

"Yep, this is where we small-town types go to see and be seen," Andrea drawled in her best country-hick imitation. "Walmart, basketball games, and the funeral home. Ack!" Without warning she halted the cart, slamming them both into it. She whipped the cart toward the toy section.

"What—?"

"Callie, stay with me." Andrea's voice morphed into panic. "I'll explain in a minute."

Intrigue during her first week in Plymouth? Callie hadn't counted on that. Andrea guided them behind a huge wire bin of bright-colored beach balls and peeked around its edge.

"Um, Andrea?" *This is so not you.* "Why are we hiding? What are you looking at?"

"See that guy—"

"What guy?" Had they time-traveled back to junior high? Callie hoped Pastor Sam didn't wander this direction.

"In the Twelve-Items-or-Less line. You don't recognize him?"

Callie's contacts didn't cooperate, so she had to squint. But she recognized him, all right.

Jason Kenton.

The last person in Plymouth she'd ever want to see.

Chapter 2

Assuming the role of gopher had never been Jason's life dream.

Still, he could handle standing in a Walmart line if that would keep Grandpa resting in his recliner.

He compared Grandma's organized but shakily written list to the items in his cart, grinning at the last one, a giant blue jar. Grandma thought vapor rub could cure anything from fallen arches to chicken pox. Jason doubted Grandpa's cardiologist included it on the long list of medications Grandpa took after his heart attack. He both chuckled and winced at the mental picture of his tiny grandmother threatening his big, crusty grandfather, forcing him to follow doctor's orders.

Wish I could stay with him more. Grandma needs more breaks. But no matter how hard he tried to get along with the old man, Grandpa blew up at him. Illness hadn't mellowed him one bit. Jason wondered if Grandpa would ever let the past be the past....

As Jason reached for his billfold, an odd movement caught his attention. Out of the corner of his eye, he saw something—a nose?—poke around a pile of beach balls, then vanish. Two noses materialized and then did the disappearing act.

Trying not to laugh, Jason pulled his cart from the line and pushed it to the beach balls. A face emerged from the display to match the nose, including a pair of hostile blue eyes. He halted and the laughter died in his gut. Andrea Taylor. She was *hiding* from him? He'd tried to apologize, but—

The face beside Andrea's grabbed him, one with glittering green eyes and high cheekbones, an unusual face with sculpted features. This woman with the trendy black haircut—how could she seem familiar? Yet he knew he'd seen her before. Where? When?

He'd better wait until later to settle those questions. Right now, he needed to think survival. *God, please tell me what to do. Preferably before Andrea slugs me.*

"Hey." He offered what he hoped was a friendly smile.

How could Andrea's icy eyes shoot fire? She pushed their cart past him and turned into the pet food aisle, though he knew her family didn't own an animal. Before the other girl followed, her gaze lasered through him, scanning every thought in his head. As if she'd clicked and opened a photo file, pictures of a scrawny teen girl popped up in his mind.

Callie Creighton. Callie, with the same sermonizing look he'd tried to shrug off years ago. He'd heard that after she graduated from Notre Dame, she'd landed a top job in Chicago. Whoa, she certainly looked the part. He'd hardly recognized her at first. Why was she shopping in Plymouth?

Probably visiting Andrea. Despite different backgrounds, those two had been thick in high school. When they were teens, Callie annoyed him more than any girl he knew. Most of the time, he'd managed to keep her at a distance.

Now, watching her walk away, he realized that given a chance, he might change his mind about that.

Andrea looked madder than she had in kindergarten when Jason and Scott Douglas stole her Cabbage Patch doll. She gave no hint why she, never a drive-by-the-boy's-house-then-yell-and-floor-it type in high school, had hidden from Jason. Callie decided to delay the You-want-to-tell-me-about-this? conversation until she plied her friend with peach smoothies. After several passes through Hardware, Andrea declared an all clear. They paid for their purchases and headed for Java Trail, the downtown coffeehouse whose walls had heard their secrets since Mr. Klein's algebra class.

Yum. She hadn't enjoyed a smoothie this good in a long time. Callie stretched, every cell in her body savoring the relaxed pace of this day, the springtime sun shining on them with obvious approval through Java Trail's large windows. *Thank You, Lord, for bringing me back.*

"So-o-o nice to slow down." The coffeehouse, with its contemporary yet cozy atmosphere, seemed to give her a welcome-home hug.

"You don't want to drive back to Chicago today?" Stirring her smoothie, Andrea grinned.

"No thanks. I think I'll stay off the interstates for a few decades." Callie shifted in her chair, shrugging her shoulders. "I don't ever want to move again, either. I'm still sore from unloading my stuff."

Andrea grimaced. "You and me both. Patrick probably is, too."

"It was sweet of him to help us." Callie didn't know quiet Patrick very well, but his muscles certainly came in handy.

"When you find a job, we'll help you move your things from the storage unit to an apartment." Andrea crossed her arms. "But don't ask me to move you away from Plymouth. Ever."

Callie grinned. "Only if God informs me He's made a change of plans."

Perched on a high stool sipping her smoothie, Andrea, despite perfect makeup, looked more like a little girl than a bank officer. Her eyes no longer glittered like headlights clicked on "bright," so Callie knew her friend would tell her about Jason, maybe halfway through her drink.

Only she didn't. Andrea talked about Patrick and their wedding, her work, Plymouth's upcoming sales. She even discussed the weather, though Andrea disliked boring people who talked about the weather. She covered everything but their weird Walmart encounter with Jason Kenton.

Wow, a two-smoothie problem. Now her friend toyed with the small vase holding the purple flowers on their table and rearranged the salt and pepper shakers.

Callie bought another round of peach smoothies. Andrea chattered on and on about nothing.

When she finally took a breath, Callie's words seized the moment like the last passengers jammed into a Chicago L train: "Andrea, you were the only girl at our high school who didn't fall for Jason or his sneaky tactics. Why did he get to you today? I've never seen you so upset about one guy saying 'hi.'"

Silence. High-beam eyes again. "I'd rather not talk about it, if you don't mind."

"I do mind." Callie leaned down a little so she could look Andrea in the face. "Not just because we're best friends. I get the feeling you should talk about Jason, if not with me, certainly with Patrick."

Andrea lowered her voice. "I did tell Patrick about him."

"Then why were we hiding behind beach balls?" A tiny white-hot thread of—what?—flashed through Callie. Jealousy? *I haven't seen Mr. Hottie in ten years. When we were teens, if he looked my way twice, it was because I bugged him. Except for once...*

She didn't realize her mind had wandered back to High School Land until Andrea broke the silence. "He called you 'Lady Preacher,' didn't he?"

Hey, we're not talking about me here. Nevertheless, Callie felt a flush of embarrassment. "Yeah. He was dating my cousin Brandy, and I thought God wanted me to quote the Ten Commandments to them—or rather, at them—every chance I had."

"I tried—"

"Yes, you tried to tell me that wasn't the best approach." Callie shook her head. "I didn't believe you."

They sipped their drinks and fell silent.

Callie's stomach protested that two smoothies were a little much to swallow. Maybe this subject matter, too?

"Anyway, Jason's probably visiting relatives." Andrea's tone hammered a cork into the conversation.

O-kay. I guess we're done here. For now, anyway. Sooner or later, Andrea would spill everything. Callie shifted the conversational gears. "Tell me about your reception."

Andrea brightened. "I talked to the event planner at Swan Lake again. Everything's going to be perfect."

She sparkled as she spoke of the plans she and Patrick—and her mother—had made. Andrea didn't see her fiancé slip up behind her until he leaned down, surprising her with a kiss and a single red rose.

"Your mom said you were doing errands. I figured you'd end up here." Twinkles warmed Patrick's calm gray eyes as he pulled another chair to their table. He greeted Callie then focused on Andrea's animated face. He seemed content to smile and nod while she and Callie talked and talked about the flowers, the food, the music, and the decorations she and her mother planned to create for the tables.

Callie reported on her optimistic but cautious update from

the employment agency she'd hired. She also had applied at a temporary work agency, and her interviewer implied that her computer and media skills would land her a short-term job soon. Not that she wouldn't love sacrificing employment for a while to help Andrea with her wedding, but the school loan elephant soon would demand its huge monthly meal.

Job résumés. Wedding invitations. The Monster employment index. White roses or orchids? They chatted, teased, and laughed.

All the while, a small video, as if in the corner of a television screen, played at the edge of Callie's mind in a never-ending loop: Jason pushing the store cart toward them, those big, melting, toffee-colored eyes fastened on her, flashing the same grin that had made every girl in the high school faint like a fool…including her.

Go away, Jason. You were bad news in high school. Doesn't sound like you're good news now.

Chapter 3

"Good job on this Mozart piece, Chad." Jason slapped the student on the shoulder. "Smoother runs than last week. Be careful to relax your wrists. Put in the practice time. I know it's hard during the summer—"

"Is it ever." Chad shook his red Afro and slid music from the piano into his portfolio. "All my friends are at Warren Dunes today."

"Wouldn't mind hitting the beach, too." Jason grinned. "Sun, sand, Lake Michigan…"

"But if I want to make it into a good master's program—"

"It's the only way to go." Jason nodded. "You can do it, Chad. I'll be praying for you."

"Thanks." Chad's look of gratitude assured Jason he hadn't wasted this beautiful summer morning, either. When the head of Bethel College's music department asked him to serve as adjunct faculty, he knew he could work for God through his teaching, as well as performing. He didn't know he would learn more in one-on-one contact with his students than he taught them.

After Chad left, Jason wandered down Everest-Rohrer's summer-silent halls and paused by the chapel doors. He'd suffered through a couple of years of required services there. Yet he couldn't escape the passionate songs sung by the Christian crazies, several of whom had become his closest friends.

He couldn't escape Elijah, his roommate, either. Chuckling, Jason wandered past Manges Hall, where he'd lived for three years. How could a pagan maintain his hedonistic integrity living with such a funny, godly guy? Elijah kept the whole floor laughing, yet he openly prayed for Jason every day. Finally, during his third year at Bethel, Jason told Elijah he'd welcomed Christ into his life. His roommate organized a pack of dorm brothers who hoisted Jason onto their shoulders and dumped him into a campus pond for an involuntary baptism—then jumped in with him!

He'd never forget that shivering, laughing, mid-March celebration. His soppy, freezing friends hugged him, warm tears pouring down their cheeks.

What if Elijah hadn't befriended him? What if, after two major academic screwups elsewhere, Bethel hadn't offered him another chance? *Thanks, Lord, for never giving up on me. For sending me where I would find You.*

His cell rang. The youth pastor at his church asked him to play and speak at a teen event in the fall. How he would fit more into his crazy schedule, only the Lord knew. But he'd love to help rescue these kids before they made the mistakes he had.

He drove off the Bethel campus in Mishawaka, crossed one street into South Bend, its larger twin city, and headed to nearby Notre Dame.

On this muggy June day, the imposing campus looked almost empty. Its network of sidewalks tempted him to forget work. *Gotta bring my roller blades next time.* Before he moved in with his grandparents after Grandpa's heart attack, Jason had lived in South Bend, spending cool summer mornings and evenings zooming around all three campuses where he taught. Today, however, he'd better move it, or he'd be late. Sure enough, Rajan waited for him at the front door of Crowley Hall.

"Not hard to find a practice room today. Normal people are out having fun in the sun."

"Normal people don't become great musicians." Jason grinned.

He worked first with Rajan and then with another student who also wanted a head start in preparing for next year's recitals. Afterward he drove to Indiana University South Bend, where he was studying for his master's. He taught for an hour at the Fine Arts Building—one great lesson and one that made him want to plug his ears.

Jason put in a full afternoon of practice. Memorizing Rachmaninoff piano concertos wasn't for wimps, but he loved every minute, powering the resonating octaves and chords of one movement off the practice room's walls, letting a haunting lyrical movement sing through his rippling fingers. Finally he improvised sweet jumpin' jazz and finished with a half hour of vocal exercises. Though he didn't feel qualified to teach voice, the workout kept him in good shape to sing at his gigs.

He always procrastinated making the shift from music to his shift at Starbucks. Jason dashed to the parking lot, revved his temperamental little sports car, a reminder of worse but more prosperous days, and grabbed a burger at a drive-through on his way to Erskine Village.

After communing with Rachmaninoff all afternoon, he hated this car. Its engine sounded like a percussion section gone psycho. Maybe after playing the wedding shower gig Friday, he could afford to fix the muffler.

Playing for parties helped fuel him and his car. He performed schmaltzy songs for wedding festivities and national anthems for sports events, even learning to sing Polish folk tunes because the large music-loving Polish population of South Bend joyously celebrated any and all holidays—and even invented a few.

Not exactly the audiences he'd planned to wow during his teen wonder years, but deep down, he liked performing for them.

He zipped into the Starbucks parking lot and grabbed his apron from the backseat. Jason dashed through the employees' door with five minutes to spare. He took his place behind the counter as barista extraordinaire for tired shoppers with sore feet and a yen for caffeine. He knew many of his customers—college students with laptops, local business people with cell phones glued to their ears, and older people from nearby neighborhoods.

Tonight Mr. and Mrs. Nowicki came for their weekly frappuccinos. Fragile little Mrs. N walked with a cane. She looked shakier than usual, her eyes suspiciously red. In asking about their family, he learned their daughter's marriage was even shakier than Mrs. N.

"Nobody wants to stay together anymore," she said sadly in her accented English. "Nobody."

When he'd sung her "Happy Birthday" two months before, she'd acted like he was a superstar. Now, since no other customers stood in line behind the Nowickis, he patted her hand and sang her a few bars of a Polish children's song, "Karuzela," or "Carousel."

Her faded blue eyes lit up. "You know that? My sisters and I sang and danced to 'Karuzela' back in Kraków."

"We sang it in our family, too." Mr. N began to hum the tune.

Mrs. N joined in, tapping her fingers on the counter. Jason fixed their frappuccinos and finished the chorus with them.

He carried the drinks as the elderly couple slowly made their way to a table, Mr. N clasping her arm tightly. Their smiles paid Jason more than the best gig he'd ever played.

"Hey, Jason." From across the room, a guy with long black hair waved his arm. Trevor Baumgartner. Once a close friend during high school, but now he'd way rather sing to the Nowickis. "Hey, Trevor."

"Man, I haven't seen you in ages. Can you sit a couple of minutes?"

"Sorry, not till my shift's over." Jason edged back to the counter.

"When's that?"

"Ten." Lying wasn't an option anymore, but he sometimes wished it was.

"I'll come back then."

Jason waved a good-bye, hoping Trevor would find something else to do tonight.

He didn't.

Jason was locking the front door when Trevor showed up. "Ready to go?"

No, he wasn't. Jason had argued with himself all evening. He didn't want to hang with him. But was he the only Christian connection Trevor had? Or maybe—just maybe—the guy had changed.

"I'm hungry." Jason's always-empty stomach was growling at woofer levels. He hoped to steer them away from the bars. "Mind if we go to Denny's?"

"You work in a restaurant, man. You didn't eat?"

"Grabbed half a muffin. A family reunion hit Starbucks after you left. Kept us hopping the rest of the evening."

"Well, okay. I like Denny's pie."

Jason followed him to the restaurant, though he fervently wished he could go home and crash.

After they'd ordered, he asked Trevor if he had written any new songs. With luck, he'd talk until Jason's willpower had been fortified with a hot meal. Trevor, as full of himself as Jason had been, talked on and on. He'd made it more than halfway through his dinner when the real issue surfaced.

"Jason, I've saved the best for last." Trevor's black eyes glowed. "Our band is playing major gigs around the football games and Christmas and New Year's. Yesterday I got calls from a couple of places in Chicago. We're moving up, man."

"I'm glad for you, Trevor." He really was. Trevor, a gifted musician, worked hard on his music. He composed, arranged, practiced, and marketed 24-7, pushing other band members to do the same.

"Thanks. But Derek, our keyboard guy, is going back to school after Christmas and wants to go part-time with the band at that point. He'll leave for sure next spring. Wants to get his master's."

"You want me to warn him?" Jason grinned.

"You can try." Trevor rolled his eyes. "I don't get you guys, paying big bucks to go to school—especially when your folks won't help out."

Jason forked a bite of spaghetti into his mouth so he could think before he answered. Finally he said, "I've found that I like to teach."

"You like to work at Starbucks, too?"

If I join you, I won't have to, right? Jason almost said it. Sure, Trevor's band was going places now, but great prospects today didn't guarantee success tomorrow. Besides, that wasn't the point. Jason made himself smile. "Right now, I'm not sure what direction God wants my career to take. So I'm trying to prepare as best I can."

Trevor didn't cringe when Jason mentioned God—a first. *Whoa. Why is he being nice?*

"God knows you'll gain lots more experience playing with us." Trevor leaned forward. He flicked on his charm button, the one that worked on everyone. "We want you to play with us again, Jason. We never wanted you to leave. Before you say no, listen to me, okay?"

"I'm listening." How could he do otherwise?

"Give us a chance. That's all I'm asking. Derek can't do gigs in November and December, and we'd like you to sub. You'll get a feel for what we're doing now and bank some cash. Best of all, you'll make great music with us—no strings attached."

Jason's mouth watered. He never felt more alive than when playing for an audience. Convinced that was part of God's plan for him, he'd been trying to build connections with Christian bands, though he didn't rule out secular entertainment. Still—

"If you join us, you could focus on writing new material. We could cowrite, too."

Trevor's spell deepened as he held out the ultimate bait. The guy knew him way too well.

"We have musical chemistry, man. We always were good together."

His last words tightened around Jason like a boa constrictor. He battled to free himself from the suffocating offer. *No, Trevor. You're the best I've ever worked with, but we were not good together. Not at all.*

He knew what choice he should make. Jason put down his fork, his stomach roiling. "I'm flattered you want me. But I've changed. Jesus rescued me from myself. I love Him even more than my music—though I'm loving the music in a whole new way—"

"Yeah, yeah." Trevor swore. "No Jesus spiel, okay? I heard it way too much when you first became a Bethel Bible-thumper—"

"I did get carried away then." Jason shook his head.

Trevor snorted. He stood, raising his voice so that other patrons stared. "You think you've got it together now? I'd better let you and Jesus finish your spaghetti."

Before he left, Trevor leered over his shoulder. "If you ever decide to be yourself, Jason, let me know."

Chapter 4

Callie couldn't avoid the north side of downtown forever. Though she'd love to try.

Andrea didn't help matters much. When Callie collected her bag from the closet in the Taylors' enormous, echo-y foyer, Andrea crept up behind her and intoned in a deep horror-movie voice, "Sooner or later, you'll have to face The Place. *Ooooo-wahahaha.*"

Callie stuck her tongue out at her chuckling friend and headed for her car. She gave herself a pep talk. *It's really no big deal. You need to do this. Grow up, Callie.*

Still, first things first. Her thick hair was making her crazy. Thank heaven, Rhonda had room in her schedule when she'd called.

Hundreds of young corn plants waved at Callie from green fields on both sides of the road as she drove north to Plymouth. Stately trees and venerable homes that lined South Michigan Street greeted her like old friends. She drove under the railroad bridge that for some reason, everyone called the viaduct, and then turned her SUV into the parking lot near the Yellow River. At sixteen, she'd failed her first driver's test here, nearly plunging her uncle's old car and the examiner over the riverbank.

"I can drive in Chicago now—Lake Shore Drive, the Loop at rush hour—I do it all," she told the other cars, slamming her door.

She didn't mention the time she'd turned the wrong way onto an I-94 exit ramp. Why burden anyone with unnecessary details?

Ten minutes early for her appointment, she gave herself a quick "welcome home" tour of downtown. She loved the authentic 1930s globe streetlights and brick planters filled with colorful petunias and geraniums lining the street. She walked past the old Rees Theater where Andrea once treated her to Saturday Smurf matinees. Harriet's, a second-time-around store, always displayed classy merchandise in a tasteful way. Callie salivated at the sight of new releases in the City Center News and Books window.

Treat's, a downtown clothing store for decades, featured a bride in its window. Like a ten-year-old, Callie paused, almost pressing her nose against the glass. What a beautiful dress. Andrea looked enchanting in her full-skirted fairy tale come true. But this one, with its sweetheart neckline, slim bodice with artistic ruching, and asymmetrical mermaid flare from the knees down looked custom-made for Callie's long, thin build.

As if I need a wedding dress. After her breakup with Ty, she wasn't sure she'd ever need one. Callie spun around and hurried back to Kay's Beauty Salon.

"Hey, girl." Rhonda gave the sparkling white smile that made everybody's day. "I heard you were back in town for good. Whatsa matta? Chicago too small?"

"Yeah, decided it didn't work for me."

Rhonda didn't realize she actually spoke the truth. After only a week in Plymouth, where buildings didn't jam the sky, Callie's city claustrophobia had begun to fade.

"Well of course. You're a hometown girl, even if you've grown up." As her strong fingers scrubbed and rinsed, Callie envied the sureness of the beautician's hands. How would it feel to know exactly what you were doing?

"Sit there." Rhonda pointed to her chair. She zipped around managing other heads of hair while she trimmed Callie's, answering her cell when it blared, kidding the mail carrier and anyone else who poked her head inside the cheerful shop. In the process, Callie heard more local news, past and present, than she would have if she'd researched at the library all day. Familiar names flew around, landing in her heart and mind like homing pigeons. Despite Callie's reservations, it felt *good* to be back in Plymouth. Hoping to delay her pilgrimage, she wished Rhonda would take her time doing her hair.

Rhonda finished early. You couldn't fault a hairdresser for being fast and good.

Now that a bad-hair day had morphed to a good one, Callie thought perhaps she could face The Place.

Still, walking under shady maples, she slowed as she approached her nemesis. Callie paused to survey the spot on North Michigan Street she would never forget if she lived to be a hundred. Here, events happened that nearly drove her away from Plymouth forever.

She stared at its everydayness, remembering that oppressively hot Blueberry Festival ten years before. No one in Plymouth had been more astounded when, standing onstage, wearing a borrowed pink evening gown and extra makeup to cover a huge pop-up-for-the-occasion zit, she heard her name announced over the crackling loudspeaker as Miss Blueberry, beating out not only Andrea but Callie's cousin Brandy, who had assured most of Plymouth she would win.

On a sweaty Labor Day morning, she'd ridden on the Miss Blueberry parade float with her court—Brandy, in her spectacular jade green dress, still glowering at Callie—to this very spot on Michigan Street. More than twenty thousand people watched the float pass. A small but dense gray cloud of guilt about winning had followed Callie since the moment last year's winner set the rhinestone tiara on her head. *Me? Miss Blueberry?*

As hundreds of little girls oohed and aahed, the cloud vanished. With everything in her, Callie sought to follow the contest manual's admonition to represent the spirit of Miss Blueberry with "genuineness, friendliness, and enthusiasm." Spotting the judges' stand, which also held the mayor and high county officials, she summoned her very best smile and waved vigorously. Forgetting where she stood, she teetered on her unfamiliar stilettos, took a step backward, and fell off the float.

Either she kept her eyes closed or she'd repressed everything. She couldn't, however, forget her own scream or those of the Blueberry princesses, the *thud* of her back and head smacking the pavement, or the ominous blare of approaching trombones, whose players, consumed by the patriotic fervor of "The Stars and Stripes Forever," stopped only seconds before running her over.

A photographer from the *Pilot News*, hoping for a pretty-girl picture, captured her humiliation in exquisite detail in a photo that not only made the *Pilot's* front page but showed up in the *South Bend Tribune*, blasting the sophisticated image she'd tried, as a freshman, to sell to her Notre Dame buds. Chuckling friends had sent her copies for weeks, long after the physical bruises had faded. She'd looked like a june bug—in formal dress—on its back, struggling to get up.

Now standing in silence, Callie didn't realize she'd shut her eyes again until the blank, gray after-video effect of her memories misted away. Slowly she raised her eyelids, half afraid trombones would attack again. Instead, the sun, escaping sullen clouds, shone on her.

It really was no big deal. Ten years had passed. So far, not one person in Plymouth had mentioned her humiliation.

But this infamous spot told only the last chapter of her Plymouth tale. She needed to face the rest of the story, and the sooner, the better.

Callie wished she'd left the SUV at the nearby park, rather than drive into the trailer court. Would she leave with it intact? But she didn't want to walk the road, lined by dozens of mobile homes, alone.

She shook herself. This wasn't Chicago, and it was broad daylight.

She turned left before a pizza place and swung right along the northernmost border of the court and parked. She locked the car and scanned the too-familiar scene. Some mobile homes looked attractive and tidy. Others…Callie's heart sank at the sight of the dilapidated green trailer she'd once called home. Her mother had died of cirrhosis soon after they'd moved in. Callie and her dad had lived there until he died when she was twelve. The place hadn't changed much. Tired-looking trash still filled the tiny yard where three small children played. When their rubber ball bounced into the street, Callie retrieved and tossed it back before they dashed into the road.

She hadn't seen the inside of the trailer since Dad's funeral. Callie shuddered. She didn't want to.

The large, gold mobile home next door, where she'd lived afterward with Aunt Sheila, Uncle Alan, and Brandy, looked better. Apparently Aunt Sheila still bullied Uncle Alan until he mowed the grass and painted the deck and lattice skirting. A big black pot of marigolds brightened the picture. Their cheerful, fuzzy yellow heads nodded at Callie, lifting her spirits. Maybe connecting with her family again wouldn't prove as difficult as she thought. *Please help me, Lord. I believe this is one big reason You sent me back to Plymouth.* She boldly mounted steps to the deck and knocked on the metal screen door.

The pulsing roar of music within rattled the windows. A large window air conditioner, supported by scrap-lumber legs, grumbled as if mightily displeased.

After banging several times, she called Aunt Sheila on her cell. Her aunt's ringtone must have resembled a siren, because she picked up. Callie held the phone a foot from her ear. Callie's dad had said her aunt's voice could pierce four feet of steel. He was oh, so right. "Where are you?"

Callie shouted into her cell, "I'm on your deck."

"What? You forgot where we live, maybe?"

"No, Aunt Sheila." She almost screamed the words. Teens working on a wheelless rusty truck across the street stopped and stared. Two half-dressed girls draped across the hood gave her the standard bored gaze. One hulking guy looked at Callie as if she were a steak. She turned and, summoning all her vocal strength, shrieked, "I'm standing on your deck. Could you come outside?"

"Turn that noise down, Brandy. I can't hear your cousin."

Swearing ensued over Callie's cell, even louder than the music. She'd forgotten the classic endless duel carried on by her relatives: Brandy's heavy metal versus Aunt Sheila's country western. Miraculously, the door opened. Brooks, Dunn, and Reba wailed out "Cowgirls Don't Cry" at levels that should have blown the door off. Metallica's "The God That Failed" battled for a close second in the sound war.

"Well don't stand out there in the heat, girl. Come on in." Aunt Sheila, her generous hourglass body stuffed into tight rhinestone-studded jeans, grabbed Callie's hand in a death grip. Before she could explain that it was a beautiful day and she'd *love* to sit on the deck, Aunt Sheila yanked her inside.

Taking in the mobile home's cigarette-smoke-filled air felt like breathing a solid, but Callie, trying not to gag, hugged her aunt. Six years. She'd sent Christmas cards and gifts and risked her hearing by calling. Occasionally she'd sent money. But the last time she saw her aunt had been her surprise appearance—resplendent in shocking pink sequins—at Callie's Notre Dame graduation.

"Well look at you. Skinny as ever."

Callie turned. Brandy, who always seemed to be posing, stood at the end of the hallway. She swung her thick, black waist-length french braid over her shoulder. Her smoky gray-green eyes, lighter than Callie's, scanned her like an x-ray machine.

Gorgeous. Everyone said her cousin had inherited the looks in the family. The old bag-of-bones feeling seeped through Callie. She tried to keep her voice cordial. "You haven't changed a bit, Brandy. How are you?"

"I'm just wonderful." Her cousin crossed the cramped living room, flopped onto the sofa, and lit a cigarette. "Peachy-keeno. I love my job. *Love* this town."

Callie knew she'd been working at a convenience store. "I'm sorry I couldn't find you a job in my agency, Brandy."

"I know you tried so-o-o hard."

Every word Brandy said rang like a bell out of tune. Callie fought to keep from returning the favor: *Not many positions listed "expert shoplifter" as a qualification. Your probation didn't help a lot, either.* Instead, she said, "I'm unemployed right now; if I see a job that might work for you, I'll let you know."

"Thanks so much." Brandy rolled her eyes.

Callie longed to escape. *I need a run. Maybe to Chicago.*

"Sit down awhile." Aunt Sheila straightened her ugly afghan on the back of a worn chair. "Want a diet cola? A beer?"

"Just a glass of ice water, please." Her aunt was making an

effort to connect. While Aunt Sheila, upon finding no beer in the refrigerator, argued with Brandy about who paid for the last case, Callie sat and tried to dredge up a safe conversational topic.

Not Uncle Alan. He'd probably drunk the last several six-packs.

Not her aunt's job. A nursing home aide, she and her boss did not get along.

Brandy stormed out of the room. Aunt Sheila handed Callie a glass of water. She gulped it down as Metallica roared and groaned from the back bedroom.

"I love the marigolds on your deck," Callie said at last.

"Thanks. I bought them for myself on Mother's Day." Aunt Sheila's gaze followed Brandy's exit route, stabbing the hallway like a sharp sword.

Guess that wasn't a safe topic. Callie looked longingly toward the door, the access to sunshine, quiet, and oxygen.

"If that girl doesn't move out soon, we're going to kill each other." Aunt Sheila swept her lethal gaze to Callie, pinning her to the chair. "I suppose Alan would like that. Then he could drink all day *and* all night."

Please don't do this again. You were kind to me, but you used me as your sounding board. For six years, I listened to you dissing your husband. Dissing your daughter. No wonder Brandy always resented me.

When Aunt Sheila finally stopped to breathe, Callie said gently, "I know you're unhappy. I was, too. But Jesus changed me—"

"Great." Her aunt stuffed a cigarette into her mouth. "You've gone and got religion *again*? I thought you gave all that up." She lit it and shook her head, exhaling the smoke with a snort. "I should never have let you go to that church. But the cute youth pastor was so nice. He brought us a turkey every Christmas. A ham, too."

"Pastor Dustin introduced me to Christ, but Jesus was the one who helped me. He helps me now." *I've tried to explain a thousand times.* Callie had used every persuasive power she'd learned in advertising. *Why don't you get it?*

"I wish churches would just help everyone and forget all that stuff that makes people mad." Aunt Sheila rummaged once more in the refrigerator, discovering a beer that had escaped Uncle Alan's unerring homing instinct. She held its frostiness against her red, angry face and then popped the top.

"You want to forget about Jesus?" Callie asked.

She could almost read her aunt's mind: a vague recall of long-ago Bible-school lessons and once-a-decade Christmas sermons. "Well no. I wouldn't want to do that. He was a good man—all about healing people, wasn't He? Everybody knows He was a great teacher."

"He was," Callie said. "But He was much more than that. Jesus claimed to be the Son of God." Callie leaned forward. "Aunt Sheila, a man who says He is the Son of God either *is* divine—or He was crazy. Or He must have been smoking something pretty potent."

Her aunt's jaw dropped. Reba and Metallica sang halfway through another chorus of their respective songs before she could talk. Finally she said, "Callie Sue Creighton, I can't believe what you just said. I've heard terrible things come out of my own daughter's mouth, but she doesn't say Jesus was a pothead. What kind of religion are you following, anyway?"

"Aunt Sheila, that's not what I meant—"

Her aunt rose from the sofa, her hand to her forehead. "I don't know what this younger generation is thinking. Just stop, okay?"

"Okay." Chewing her lip, Callie didn't know what else to say. But that didn't present a problem. Aunt Sheila, her tongue loosened by the beer, told Callie exactly what she thought of those politicians in Washington.

For a half hour, Callie nodded and tried to smile. Then she kissed her aunt, threw a good-bye down the hall to Brandy's closed door, and left, wondering why she'd thought she could make a difference here.

"Austin! Desiree!" Standing in Eastside's crowded foyer with Andrea and Patrick, Callie threw her arms around the beaming teens. "Can it really be you?"

"Of course it's me." Red-headed Austin, who had grown at least two feet since she'd last seen him, gave her his familiar freckle-faced grin. "Don't I look the same?"

Callie tilted her head back. "You'll always be a teddy bear. But I have to look *up* to you now?"

"You still don't have to look up to me." Desiree, a shy six-year-old when Callie first brought her to church, had matured into a petite young woman with a quiet but confident smile.

"You're all grown-ups. How am I supposed to handle this?"

Austin gestured with his Bible. "The same way you always told us to handle everything. Give it to God."

Hearing him quote her own words made Callie feel like a million dollars. "Well that doesn't change, does it?"

"They're both on the youth committee." Andrea celebrated the reunion with more hugs. "These two are out to change the world."

"Or at least, Plymouth High School." Desiree grinned, but Callie noticed she set her jaw the same way she had as a little girl.

"We've been inviting kids from our trailer park to church, of course. Just like when you brought us. We're gonna do puppets at the Blueberry Festival and tell kids about Jesus." Austin waved across the room at a smiling young man with a shaved head, grabbed Callie's arm, and dragged her with him. "Hey, Eric. I want you to meet somebody."

Austin bumped knuckles with the guy. "This is Eric

Schwartz, the greatest youth pastor in the world. Eric, this is Callie. She's the one who brought me to church when I was a little kid."

"Hi, Eric." Callie liked the young man's kind eyes and open face. "I'm so glad Austin and Desiree have a friend like you." *A better friend than I was. I should have looked them up on Facebook.*

"We're really glad she came back home." Andrea, who had followed, slipped her arm around Callie.

"All of us are glad." Desiree did the same.

"Looks like you have a fan club." Eric grinned. Glancing at the two teens, he clasped her hand. "Thanks for introducing Austin and Desiree to the Lord."

She couldn't answer for the lump of joy in her throat. But she didn't have to because the pipe organ's prelude in the sanctuary ended, and the introduction to the first hymn propelled everyone through the doors and into the back pews—except Eric. A sudden blur, he zoomed down the side aisle to a seat near the front.

"New world's record for the Sunday morning dash," whispered Austin, sitting next to Callie.

She threw a smile at him and at Andrea on her left, who returned it. Dustin, the youth pastor when Callie and her friends attended as teens, ran the same race every week.

So good to be at Eastside! Callie occasionally visited churches in Chicago, but never seemed to connect.

Quieting her heart, she sang the words of an old hymn with the congregation. Austin's booming baritone reminded her of the tune: "Be Thou my vision, O Lord of my heart, naught be all else to me, save that Thou art...."

Lord, my vision's pretty cloudy right now. I need to focus on You and Your purpose for me in Plymouth.

Immediately her visit at Aunt Sheila's, in all its loud, smoky misery, played across her mind. She almost groaned aloud. *How did I stand it for six years?*

Mostly to escape the scene, she glanced sideways at Austin and Desiree, their young faces consumed with worshipping God. They were growing up in similar circumstances. But God had used her to help rescue them, just as Andrea and the Taylors had rescued her.

"Heart of my own heart, whatever befall, Still be my vision, O ruler of all."

What is God's heart?

A vision of the teenagers fixing the truck rose before her. The little ones playing in her former home's trashy yard. Dozens of kids lived in those trailer courts—big, little, some cared for, many not.

Dozens who didn't know Jesus.

I'm listening, Lord. Tell me more.

Callie had shared an office with characters, even an animal or two. But never with a brown cow.

"People bring their kids here to see Cocoa." Marsha, the receptionist at Hometown Dairy, Callie's new temporary employer, patted the life-sized figure's back. "She's great PR."

"I'm sure she is." Pasting on a bright smile, Callie sat at the desk Marsha indicated. "But aren't there plenty of real cows around for them to pet?" *This thing takes up half the office. I feel like Cocoa's practically looking over my shoulder.*

"Sure, but most of them won't let kids sit on their backs." Marsha sidestepped the fiberglass figure in order to fetch papers from her boss's office. She caught Callie's incredulous glance. "You'll get used to Cocoa. Before long, you won't notice her any more than a file cabinet."

File cabinets didn't have horns. Or long-lashed, dead-looking eyes. Or a shiny, bulging pink udder.

Oh well. Working part-time at this temp job, she could

handle a fake cow as an office colleague. After all, she'd dealt with Mr. Stonewell for six years.

She turned back to her desk and checked out the computer. Fortunately, it looked up-to-date with programs she'd used before. She reviewed material Marsha had e-mailed her and acquainted herself with the company's sales files. Not well organized, but bearable. For the remainder of the morning, she immersed herself in facts and figures and listed ideas for a new brochure her elderly boss, Mr. Carlyle, had discussed with her.

Her dry mouth reminded her she hadn't left her desk since Marsha took her on the initial office tour. Time for a coffee break. Still pondering possibilities, she turned, half rising from her desk, only to plant a kiss squarely on Cocoa's hard black nose.

She barely managed to keep from falling back onto her desk. Fortunately, she let out only a mouselike squeal, probably inaudible to Mr. Carlyle, whose door was shut. Marsha routinely took an early lunch hour, so only she and Cocoa herself witnessed the undignified encounter. Rubbing her mouth, Callie maneuvered past the statue and headed for the coffee area in back.

First day on the job, and I kiss a cow. She stirred double cream into her cup and, giggling a little, watched her step as she returned to her desk. "Sorry, no kiss this time, Cocoa."

She tried to focus on work, but she couldn't shake the absurd somebody's-watching-me sense that Cocoa's presence gave her.

Before long, she realized she couldn't have concentrated anyway. A gray-haired, blue-jeaned man named Mr. Drummond entered with two small children and told her he had an appointment with Mr. Carlyle.

She checked the schedule and buzzed her boss, assuming the man would take the kids with him.

Instead, he patted their curly dark heads and said, "Want to ride the cow?"

"Yeah!" They dashed to Cocoa as Mr. Drummond disappeared into Mr. Carlyle's office. The little boy scaled the figure like Mount Everest. Callie leaped from her desk just in time to save him from a fall.

"Grandpa said I could ride her." He looked at Callie as if she'd insulted him.

For a half hour she rescued and re-rescued the climbers between phone calls. She helped them take turns sitting on the cow's back and calmed them with Cocoa adventure stories she invented. Actually, she would have enjoyed her babysitting stint if she hadn't worried about delayed progress on the report Mr. Carlyle wanted by the week's end. Also, nothing in her education had prepared her for answering the little ones' endless questions.

"Are you married?"

"Do cows get married?"

"What's that?" The boy pointed.

"That's uh, an udder." Absurd that she should feel her face redden.

"Do people have udders, too?"

Only Mr. Drummond's appearance saved her from having to answer that one. Mr. Carlyle beamed at her as if she'd upped the company's profits. He left with Mr. Drummond and company for lunch. When Marsha returned, she confirmed that he expected them to "mix with" visitors, including doing Cocoa duty with their children. "He thinks it confirms Hometown Dairy's image as a friendly, family sort of place."

After six years in Chicago, Callie thought she knew the ropes when it came to PR.

Even Mr. Stonewell might learn something new here.

Chapter 5

Jason glanced around the large room at the Swan Lake resort with its fussy, flower-decked tables and fourteen-fork table settings. When his parents visited from Texas, they occasionally dragged him to fancy places, but years of burgers between classes and jobs had cured him of any yen for elaborate froufrou.

Still, he liked playing for gigs like this, froufrou and all, because he felt he was contributing to a special moment in a person's life. Jason ran his fingers over the baby grand piano's smooth black-and-white keys, listening to its rich resonance. They always kept the pianos tuned here. He wouldn't have to spend the evening faking a smile while playing nails-on-a-blackboard notes.

A new server, setting up more tables, paused to listen. "You're good."

"Thanks." Hoping the party attendees would think the

same, Jason placed a couple of dollars in his crystal tip jar beside the piano's music rack.

He sipped coffee while he reviewed the battle plan for the evening. The resort's event planner told him the guests would mingle and then eat. He would supply background music until after dinner, taking a break while they played corny shower games. He'd probably resume his duties while the bride-to-be opened her presents, keeping an eye open for gag gifts and sentimental heirloom moments.

But Jason wouldn't know the actual plan until whoever was giving the shower added her two cents'—or, as it often turned out, her twenty dollars'—worth of suggestions. Fortunately, he'd memorized dozens of love songs. His listeners rarely stumped him, which often led to generous tips and great recommendations.

Women of all ages attended wedding showers, so he reviewed both favorites from the past and contemporary songs. He was playing the opening bars of "It Had to Be You" when Callie Creighton walked in. Her green-star eyes widened as if a music-loving alien had dropped from the sky.

His fingers forgot their place in the song.

Jason Kenton?

One second, Callie wished Andrea were here to drag her behind a Walmart beach ball display.

Two seconds later, Callie thanked the Lord she was not.

Jason was playing for Andrea's shower? Why? His parents had almost as much money as Andrea's.

"May I help you, Ms. Creighton?" The head server materialized at her elbow.

"Um, no. Yes. Maybe later."

Despite Callie's angst, Jason looked so handsome in that sand-colored suit she'd almost tripped over her tongue. Had she drooled? He must think…

Who cared what he thought? Callie strode across the room, hoping all the planning had finally driven her over the edge. Maybe she was hallucinating.

"Hello." Jason had placed his hands in his lap, looking every inch the professional entertainer. "I take it you're in charge. Do you have instructions for the evening?"

"Instructions?" Shaking her head, she let her hands fall limp to her sides. "What are you doing here? I don't know what Andrea has against you, but we both know she will freak when she sees you." *Twenty minutes. She'll arrive in twenty minutes.*

"So Andrea is the bride-to-be." Though he held his composure, a shadow darkened his eyes. "To answer your question, this is my job. The event planner contacts another pianist or me to play for Swan Lake parties."

"Then I'll ask her to call the other guy." Callie turned on her heel.

"She's a girl, and she's out of town. Actually, I wasn't supposed to play tonight; she switched dates with me. She does it all the time."

Words came to Callie's mind, a vocabulary from her past she'd tried to forget. One more reminder that entering Plymouth's city limits didn't change her. *Lord, forgive me. I so want this to be perfect for Andrea.* She surveyed the room with its sea-blue tablecloths and fanned napkins, gleaming silver, and lovely bridal white flowers. A scene that would explode the minute Andrea saw Jason. *Maybe we'd better forget the music.*

But Andrea, excited to have a pianist for her shower, had asked for specific songs. Even if Callie fired Jason, she'd have to explain why—and mess with her best friend's magic evening. What would Callie say? What should she do?

He rose from the bench. "I think we can work this out."

"How?" She poured all her frustration into the word. "Just how are you going to fix this?"

He paused and then shook his head. "I can't. I can't fix it."

Honesty. Regret. Callie stared at him. Neither characteristic had been Jason's strong point.

"I can only make a suggestion or two." He gestured at the piano. "We'll shift it so I won't sit under the lights. Then we'll move one of those big flower arrangements in front of me so I'll fade into the background."

"You? Fade into the background?" She blurted the words out before she thought.

He smiled. "I do a great Muzak imitation. Most people don't even see waiters or musicians."

"What if Andrea walks up to you with a request? What if—"

"I'll disappear whenever I can. But you'll have to keep her away. Tell her she's the queen of the evening, that she shouldn't lift a finger. You can bring her requests to me."

He made it sound like a sane plan. Besides, did she have a choice?

"All right." She gestured to the head server and asked him to help Jason.

"Move the piano?" The man looked less than thrilled.

"Move the piano." Callie added Chicago edge to her voice. "Don't worry. We're not dragging it to the other end of the room, just shifting it toward the wall and a little sideways."

He reluctantly gathered the other servers around the imposing instrument. Jason shed his coat.

Callie crossed the room to the entrance and grabbed one of the two large bouquets of roses, lilies, and ivy flanking the door. Having watched Jason and the servers, with mighty grunts, shift the piano, she repositioned the bouquet and its tall stand in front of the bench. She then stationed herself at the front table, where Andrea would sit.

Jason wiped sweat from his face. "What do you think?"

What did she think? Sweat, like everything else, looked good on him. Feeling her cheeks heat, she shoved the thought aside. "Moving the piano helped. But if anything, the flowers draw attention to you. Small bushes or large plants would work better. I remember seeing them in the hallways." She glanced at her watch. "I'll tell the event planner later I borrowed their greenery."

"I'll help you look."

She dashed down the hallway with Jason, almost giggling as he spirited away a spreading palm from a spot near the men's room. How had they morphed into fellow conspirators? With the clock ticking, she didn't take time to think about their strange alliance. She borrowed two lush, smaller plants from an end table by a chair. Together they hauled their booty to the party room. Jason donned his coat and resumed his position on the bench while she arranged plants.

"I should have worn camo instead of a suit." For the first time, he offered his devastating high school grin—the one that captured her as a teen, though she scorned him as a sinner.

Her heart beat like a snare drum. Ridiculous. Callie fixed her attention on the plants then stepped back several paces to survey the results. "Better. Still—" She pushed the pots around and fiddled with palm branches. "Yes. With the palm shifted to the side and branches hiding your face, the effect's more subtle than the flowers. I think that will work."

She handed him the list of songs Andrea wanted and a couple for the toasts. "Do you know these?"

He skimmed them. "Sure."

Beads of perspiration dribbled down her face, and she wondered if her new dress smelled like she'd worked out at the gym. He still emanated his woodsy aftershave fragrance. Not fair.

None of this was fair. *Jason, you'd better not ruin Andrea's evening.*

She snapped, "Just don't give yourself away, okay?"

"I'm completely at your service."

She caught her breath, falling under the spell of that oh-so-smooth voice, those melting toffee eyes... .

Callie hurried off, wishing he looked the part of a fairy-tale villain.

Playing behind the green facade, Jason felt like a musical George of the Jungle. Callie hadn't realized that in hiding him, she'd minimized his tip-earning potential. But he had to think positive. At first sight, she'd looked ready to throw him out. This way, he'd earn a full evening's pay. The event planner wouldn't blow up at him for antagonizing a client and scratch him off her entertainers list. As long as Andrea didn't realize who was playing love songs while she finished her chicken cordon bleu, he remained safe.

He permitted himself to glance Andrea's way. He'd heard she was marrying a solid Christian guy; she looked happy tonight, and he celebrated with her. Even as self-centered as he'd been during their brief fling, he couldn't miss her invisible bruises. Now, playing her grandmother's request, "Some Enchanted Evening," he prayed God would bless Andrea and Patrick.

His fingers spelled out the melody and chords as naturally as he spelled his name. A little bummed at first by his leafy disguise, he decided to enjoy this arrangement. On a regular night, he deliberately sought the eyes of individual listeners. Establishing rapport made the difference between an empty tip jar and a full one. Tonight he didn't have to smile unless he felt like it. Watching Callie, he felt like it.

Teetering a little on funky high-heeled sandals that somehow looked elegant, she wore a simple bright green dress that drew its color from her eyes. Her short black hair stood up all over her head like a kitten's at play. Sitting beside Andrea, she transfused joy from her friend. Andrea was happy. Ergo, Callie was, too.

Until she overturned a water pitcher on the beverage table. An odd mixture of awkwardness and grace, that girl. As Jason played James Blunt's "You're Beautiful," he puzzled for the millionth time about what made a woman lovely. Callie didn't possess classic features, and some men would think her too thin. Yet what guy wouldn't notice her?

Having helped the server clean up her mess, Callie, now sporting wet spots on her front, made hostess rounds of the room. She talked mostly to quiet guests, those who looked as if they felt outside the ring of teasing and laughter.

She headed his direction, and he dropped his eyes to his hands.

"Andrea's mother wants 'You're Just Too Good to Be True,'" she whispered. "Do you know it?"

"Oh yeah." He kept his voice casual, though his heart rate spiked at the curve of her creamy cheek and full red mouth, the citrusy scent of her standing close to him.

When she turned to walk away, he wanted to say, "Don't go." He kept quiet, though, and watched her tall figure return to her table. Jason hummed along, realizing he, like the lyricist, couldn't take his eyes off this girl.

He'd asked God to keep Andrea focused on her party. Maybe he should have prayed about his own wandering vision. His gaze dropped to his fingers again, though they needed no guidance.

He'd also promised God he'd minimize the girl-watching. But tonight was nothing like the endless meat-market inspections he'd conducted before he'd given his life to Christ. In watching Callie, he admired her as God's living work of art.

The town grapevine said that she'd returned to Plymouth

for good. Though Callie and he hadn't exactly clicked so far, he dared hope the gossips had it right.

Now she was rising to toast her friend. "I've heard sisters share close relationships, though I never had one." Callie paused, a quiver in her voice. "Andrea, you are my sister in Christ. Though we've clashed at times, and I haven't appreciated you as I should, no biological sister could be closer to me." A crystal tear escaped from her eye. "I wish you and Patrick the best blessings the Lord can give." She raised her glass. "To Andrea and Patrick."

"Andrea and Patrick," the women echoed, clinking glasses. They dissolved in a contradictory shower of tears and giggles.

As he played, he missed his old Bethel roommate, Elijah. His brother in Christ now served as a missionary in South America. Would they ever toast each other's joy this way?

Callie wasn't finished. As Jason played "Wind beneath My Wings," she extended a hand to Andrea's mother. "Lana, you have been like the mother I lost. If it hadn't been for you and Rich, I—I don't know what I would have done."

No wonder she and Andrea were so close. Jason hadn't understood the role the elder Taylors had played in her life. His eyes moistened again. His loving parents had encouraged him to go to youth group, but they rarely attended church themselves. They hadn't given him the solid spiritual ground that might have kept him out of trouble.

Laughter, squeals, and a few catcalls brought him back to the present. He recognized the signal: time for all guys to leave. He rounded off his song. Before he could slip away, however, a woman entered modeling a mud-ugly flannel nightgown, curlers, and a green, gooey face masque. Guests unrolled massive amounts of toilet paper. Some guy in Scooby-Doo pajamas jumped out of an enormous purple cake.

Definitely time to take a break.

* * *

Andrea opened the silver box, letting the wrapping drop to the floor. While she exclaimed about the white quilt inside, Callie, who had been recording gifts beside her, grabbed the poufy blue ribbon and stapled it onto a paper plate with five others.

"Six! Judging by this bunch of ribbons, you and Patrick had better buy a *big* house."

Andrea flung curls over her shoulder. "I am not having six kids. Patrick knows the max is four."

Callie grinned. "Uh-huh. I remember in high school you said you'd never marry—"

"You look innocent, but you really have a mouth on you, you know?"

In answer, Callie tied the paper plate on her friend's head. *"Ta-daaaaa!"*

While Andrea paraded around and posed for the cameras, Callie shot a glance toward the piano, hoping Jason would catch the hint. Why hadn't he left? He could have slipped out several songs ago. Anchored to her spot because she was recording gifts, she couldn't steal away to send him home. Anyway, only a few more gifts remained.

Then she could take a huge, relieved breath and rejoice because her best friend appeared to have had the time of her life at her wedding shower. Just enough elegance. Just enough pizzazz. Just enough craziness…and perfect music. Smooth at exactly the right time. Rhythmic and fun at exactly the right time, as if Jason had read Callie's mood for the evening and followed her lead.

Andrea hammed it up to "Get Me to the Church on Time," using a newly acquired marble rolling pin in place of a microphone. Afterward, Callie hauled her back to her gifts and got her on task.

Now Jason played a familiar melody, but she couldn't think

of the lyrics. A gentle, even slightly haunting piece, it seemed the perfect music to end the shower, reminding them all of the sweetness of this moment, one that soon would pass. The notes swirled around Callie like a long silk ribbon. She felt it drawing her back, back to Jason's corner....

Andrea stiffened beside her, and the magic vanished.

"That's 'Think of Me.'" She bit off the words. "I can't stand that song."

She spoke in such a low tone that only Callie could hear. The other girls were yakking away, as they had throughout the shower, but she felt her friend's anger.

Andrea peered toward Jason's corner. "Who's playing the piano?"

Her voice told Callie she already had guessed, but Callie answered anyway. "Jason Kenton. The planner hired him."

"You knew this?" Andrea's eyes turned to blue ice.

"Twenty minutes before you came. I couldn't get a substitute." Sudden fatigue sapped her muscles. She fought to keep tears out of her voice. "I didn't want to mention Jason. I wanted you to have the best wedding shower in the world because you're my best friend."

"I am having the best shower in the world, and all because of you." The glaciers in Andrea's eyes began to melt, and she squeezed under Callie's arm in their usual tall-short hug. "But would you ask him to stop? Please?"

"Your wish is my command." Callie tried to recover a little of the night's fun. "I'll beam him to Neptune without delay."

"Tell him Andromeda is nice this time of year." Andrea's eyes still glittered, but a tiny smile sneaked onto her face.

Callie slipped away while her friend opened her last gift.

She felt like punching Jason just because he existed. But walking toward him, she saw sadness in his face as he muted chords and ended "Think of Me." He'd watched the whole drama play out.

For the first time, she felt sorry for Mr. Hottie.

"You don't have to tell me this." Callie shifted the trash bag filled with crumpled wrapping paper from hand to hand.

Watching servers gather dishes, Andrea lowered her voice. "Maybe I should. I've only told God and Patrick about Jason. I haven't even told my mother. With him showing up in my life again"—she gritted her teeth—"I need to get this out of my system before the wedding. But I sure don't want to discuss it with Patrick again." She spread her fingers on her temples and closed her eyes.

"Not getting a migraine, are you?" Callie hated to think of Andrea's shower ending in one of her debilitating headaches.

"Not yet. Maybe if I decompress, we'll head this off at the pass." She nodded toward the beverage table. "Let's grab iced tea and find a quiet spot."

"Outside? No, it's still pouring." Callie had delayed carrying Andrea's gifts out to her car, hoping the rain would stop soon. "I think I know where we can talk." She recalled a loveseat at the end of a nearby hallway, one she'd seen during that silly plant hunt with Jason.

As they carried drinks there, his laughing, boyish face met Callie at every corner. He hadn't meant to ruin Andrea's evening; actually, he'd helped make it memorable. Whatever he'd done to anger Andrea, she probably was overreacting again— her friend had always felt strongly about everything ranging from lima beans to the Pledge of Allegiance.

However, unless Andrea debriefed to the point of laughing off Jason's offense, Callie had better forget the brief moment or two during the evening when she'd turned to find his big-eyed gaze on her, that smile on his lips.

Finding their refuge, they collapsed onto the loveseat. Andrea kicked off her sandals and sipped her tea in silence.

Despite aching feet, Callie didn't want to remove hers. This didn't sound like the fun girl talk she'd anticipated after the shower.

Finally Andrea spoke. "Remind me to tell the event planner I do *not* want Jason playing for my reception."

"Sure." Callie agreed, though she didn't think that would be necessary.

Her friend sighed, not meeting Callie's gaze. "A few years ago, I went through a tough time spiritually. You remember, Grandma was dying—my sweet, godly grandma, who kept saying Jesus would take care of her. No one could control her pain. Of course I visited her in the hospital, though I could hardly stand to, and helped Mom take care of her. But I wondered why Jesus wouldn't heal her. Or at least, help her hurt less."

Callie squeezed Andrea's hand. *Why didn't I realize how difficult her illness was for you? Why didn't I come back—*

"Don't beat yourself up." Andrea read her mind, as usual. "I'm not sure any human being could have helped me then. I woke up every day angry at God. Really angry. I'd made good grades all my life, listened to my parents, blown away the competition in church quiz bowls, stayed sexually pure, the works." She turned to face Callie. "Why had I bothered, when God wouldn't listen to my prayers and help my grandma when she needed Him most?"

Andrea, the strong friend who had brought her to Christ and helped her grow in her faith. Andrea, who for the first time in her life, had faced a situation she couldn't handle.

"So, so hard." Callie hugged her. "I know how you feel."

"I know you do, having lost your parents." Andrea nodded, her eyes moist. "That's why I can talk to you. I hadn't met Patrick yet, so he wasn't around to prop me up. Eventually God and Pastor Sam helped me work through my anger and grief, and I could sense His love again. But in the middle of the emotional and spiritual mess, I became involved with Jason." She dropped her head. "Soon I—I found myself compromising in ways I'd never intended."

Callie said nothing. What could she say?

Andrea's face flushed with humiliation. "After years of Sunday school superstar status, I almost crashed and burned." She leaned her forehead against curled fists. "When I finally drew the line, Jason broke it off."

For a long moment Callie sat, her arm dangled across Andrea's shoulders. The almost-dormant spot of Jason-suspicion in her gut erupted into hot outrage.

Slowly Andrea raised her chin. "God has forgiven me, and so did Patrick. We talked about our histories when we first began to get serious. But tonight when I heard 'Think of Me'— Jason told me it was *our* song"—she laughed bitterly—"and saw him, my mistakes all came flooding back."

The enormous diamond solitaire glittered on her small, long-nailed hands as she twisted the edge of her skirt. "I hadn't seen him since our breakup. Why did he have to show up now?"

"I don't know." A cold, murky disappointment settled on Callie. If Andrea compromised when life got tough, how could Callie ever hope to succeed?

Even while she hugged Andrea again, she wanted to twist Jason's neck. He'd preyed upon her friend's pain.

Chapter 6

"It's so dark it's hard to tell if these clouds are rotating. But one way or t'other, this is one humdinger of a summer storm." Jason's grandpa, sitting beside him on the glider sofa, squinted at the tempest outside the spacious, dimly lit sunroom and fed a treat to the whiny poodle on his lap.

Jason nodded, glad he'd talked his grandmother into letting Grandpa stay up later. Storm watching was the one love they shared. Glowing skeletal fingers reached across the sky, clawing at each other while thunder growled and roared a scary fortissimo aria through the half-open windows. No gentle rain rhythms tonight; the storm slapped waves of water against the house, shaking the windows as if they were loose teeth.

Neither he nor Grandpa minded getting a little wet. If Grandma weren't keeping an eagle's eye watch from the kitchen, Grandpa would have sneaked outside to feel the rush.

Jason would have loved standing in the wild, cleansing wind and rain, inhaling a flood of leafy freshness as the storm lessened. But that would be like eating a forbidden piece of Grandpa's favorite sugar cream pie in front of him.

Jason glanced at his watch. Ten-thirty. He'd lined up a church concert tomorrow morning in South Bend. If he actually dragged out of bed the first time the alarm buzzed, he could easily drive there and warm up before the service.

But tonight, after his not-so-great departure from Andrea's shower, he needed to leave town. This time, Grandpa wasn't the driving force. Fortunately, his good friend, Rob, who lived near Bethel, had issued Jason his apartment key and a permanent invitation to crash overnight.

"Still driving up to South Bend?"

Jason started. He and Grandpa might not live in tune, but the old man often read his mind. "Yeah, I think so."

They sat awhile without talking. The thunder and lightning calmed somewhat, but the rain continued.

"That Mazda is no good in weather like this." Grandpa growled out his unsolicited opinion. "Can your brakes hold when it's wet? Do your windshield wipers work at all?"

Translation: I care about you. Finally Jason was beginning to understand the feeling behind what used to seem an interrogation. "Yeah. At least, the last time I checked."

Grandpa didn't say anything, but he snorted—a collective reaction which covered Jason's decrepit car; his useless devotion to music; his wasteful, rowdy lifestyle from the past; his present life of faith, which Grandpa couldn't understand any better; and Jason's haircut, regardless of its length.

He rose, patting the old man on the shoulder, and then kissed Grandma, who recited her usual dire warnings and handed him a bag of peanut butter cookies.

Though Jason's car gave him fits, right now it comprised the only good-sized piece of property he could call his own. Squinting through its rain-pocked windshield as he drove the country roads, he gave thanks for only an inch or two of water on a few low spots. No flood—yet. His stomach nagged at him like his grandparents' begging poodle. Jason hadn't eaten much at the shower. As wonderful as Grandma's cookies were, he needed a meal. So he decided to head through Plymouth and grab a burger.

Drawing near the viaduct, he saw ripples of light reflected in the dim glow of the old streetlamps shining on a puddle— no, a pond!—beneath the underpass. He slowed, about to turn off on a side street, and spotted a dark shape in the pond. A car. Jason whipped over and parked. He grabbed a flashlight from his glove compartment—some of Grandpa's ideas were worth listening to—and leaped out. Running through the rain, he shone his light toward the viaduct, spotlighting the front of a late model green Subaru with Illinois plates. A driver from out of town had plunged into the water, unaware of this occasional problem. The car practically floated.

A scream and a splash electrified him into action. He charged into the pond, frantically sweeping his flashlight beam back and forth. Dark water whooshing around his knees, he spotted movement, followed by a pair of terrified eyes. Without stopping to think, he scooped up the woman and carried her out of the flood onto higher ground. In his arms, she felt fragile as the saplings bent before the storm's bluster.

The familiar voice that spoke defied his impression. "Thank you. But I'm fine. Please put me down."

He complied and turned his flashlight in her direction.

Callie Creighton.

"Are you all right?" The guy's voice both warmed and grated against Callie's ear.

No, no, no. Staring into the flashlight's glare, she pushed back a lock of her limp, wet hair. *Please, God. Send somebody else. Send* anybody *else—*

"Um, Callie? It's Jason Kenton."

Please, just shoot me. "I know." Shivers flapped her skin like flags in the wind.

"Are you cold? I think I left a jacket in my car—"

"I—I'd appreciate that." Callie clung to her wet bag and surreptitiously tried to loosen the clinging folds of her new dress. At least she'd removed her good sandals before venturing out of her car. But why, oh why couldn't she keep her footing in that stupid water? It was only knee-deep.

His comforting arm stretched loosely across her back as they half walked, half jogged through the downpour to his car across the street. A sports car, as she'd expected. But an older model with a cracked rear window, worn-out upholstery, and a broken glove compartment catch that fell open when she yanked on the front passenger door.

"The jacket's in the trunk." He slammed her door shut.

Crumpled on the front seat along with numerous empty fast-food bags, she felt guilty because he'd gone out into the storm again. Then she remembered Andrea's revelation. *Maybe he needs a few cold showers.*

She pushed aside smashed paper cups and french fry wrappers on the floor, trying to find space in which to wedge her long bare feet. A rancid odor of onion rings attacked her nose.

As if I could criticize his car's smell. With this soppy dress, her winsome appeal resembled that of a wet sheepdog.

Appeal? Why should she worry about appealing to *him*, after the way he'd treated Andrea? Sure, he was helping right now, but how much could she trust this—this Good Samaritan?

Without warning her door opened and a windbreaker flew in, followed by a blinding beam.

Please, I don't need a spotlight. Squinting, she held up her hand. "Thanks so much."

"Oh. Sorry." He lowered the flashlight.

Gratefully she threw the jacket, broadcasting its woodsy

aftershave fragrance, around her shoulders. He loped around the front of the car and jumped into the driver's seat.

"Should I try to start your car?"

"Really, you've done enough." *Quite enough.* Sure, he'd rescued her, but he'd messed with Andrea's life and complicated Callie's day beyond imagination. She cleared her throat. "I'm afraid my phone's wet. But if you'll let me use yours, I'll try to call the Taylors again."

She hated to phone them. Andrea and Patrick had gone out of town, so Callie probably would drag her parents out of bed. "Even before I dumped my cell into the drink, it didn't seem to work. Maybe the storm knocked out a tower."

He leaned toward her. "I'm already here, so I may as well try."

She leaned back toward the car door. "The water's getting deeper by the minute—"

"I might get wet, right?"

Sitting in the shadows she couldn't see him clearly, but she felt the sizzle of his grin's electricity.

"Okay, try it. Thanks." She dug hastily into her yucky waterlogged bag and handed him her keys.

He plunged out into the rain and sloshed back to her car. Another surge of guilt washed over her, but serving as his chief spectator wouldn't help much.

She peered into the back of his car, partially lit by the streetlight. Crates of worn songbooks and piles of music filled the seat. *This isn't a car. It's a messy mobile music library.*

As long as she stayed in critique mode, she wouldn't have to think about his kindness—and what she would say when he returned, when they would have to write yet another miserable chapter together of the "Miss Blueberry Returns to Plymouth" saga.

She let her head fall back on the seat and closed her eyes. Cocoa duty, employment agency appointment, wedding shower preparations, clean up, car breakdown in the rain. Enough excitement in one day for any person, right? But no-o-o. She had to deal with Jason Kenton, too…twice.

The driver's door swung open. Callie, who'd dozed off, almost screamed.

"Hey, it's just me." He jumped in, slammed the door shut, and faced her. His wet hair stood straight up like a little boy's. Cute. A streetlight outlined his muscular shoulders and chest under his thin, wet shirt. Way more than cute.

She gulped. "You want your jacket?"

"I'm fine. Unless you're too warm."

Her temperature had risen, all right. "Uh—"

"Keep it awhile." He gestured in the direction of the viaduct. "Sorry, Callie, but your car is dead. My phone's working. If you'd like, I've got Paul's 24-Hour Towing on speed dial." Again, the felt, rather than seen, grin. "Driving this baby, I keep that number handy."

"Okay."

He handed Callie the phone and her keys. "I'll move my car closer and turn on the flashers, so we'll be visible when the truck arrives."

He coaxed the engine to life. She hadn't heard such a chorus of squeaks, rattles, and groans since her trailer court days. She waited until its cacophony morphed into an uneasy *vroom* before she called.

While she talked to Paul, fresh curiosity skipped around her mind. Jason's parents probably spent more in a day than her mother had earned waitressing in a year. Everyone knew that though his conservative grandparents never flaunted their wealth, they'd wielded considerable economic power in Plymouth for ages. Yet Jason drove this lemon and played at wedding showers to earn money. She'd also seen a Starbucks apron tossed in the back. What was with that?

He pulled over and parked. With a few shudders and knocks, the car settled into place.

She said, "Paul will be here in ten minutes."

"He'll be surprised if he actually sees my car running."

They both laughed and fell silent.

This reminded her way too much of junior high. Don't look at him. Don't *not* look at him.

She fumbled her words. "I—I forgot the viaduct sometimes floods after storms."

He shifted in his seat. "I figured that."

Yeah, he probably had. More silence. Ten minutes translated into roughly ten eternities.

Hadn't she learned any poise in the past decade? She'd prided herself on drawing out clients and making them comfortable with neutral, friendly conversation. However, after all but chasing him away from the piano at Andrea's shower, chitchat didn't seem appropriate. She couldn't very well say, "So, Jason, why are you broke? Whatever happened to being voted 'Most Likely to Wow the World?'"

He gestured at her side of the car. "I'm sorry you had to clean up the mess."

"I'm sorry I pulled you into my mess. I'm sure you have better things to do on a Saturday night."

"I don't think so."

What on earth did that mean? How was she supposed to answer?

Blinking yellow and white lights on a massive dark shadow edged up the road ahead of them. She'd never been so glad to see a tow truck in her life. Probably not as glad as Jason. Despite his remark, he probably couldn't wait to find scintillating nightlife more fun than this—with a date who actually looked like she brushed her hair.

An image of the Perfect Woman posed in her mind. Callie squashed her flat. Then rolled her eyes at her insecurity.

Why should you care, Callie? Grow up and try to make a semigraceful exit from this ridiculous situation. Although you haven't a clue how you'll get back to the Taylors'. She didn't know if he could see her face, but she glued on her best smile. "Thanks so, so much, Jason, for your help. If you hadn't come along—"

"You would have figured out something else," he said cheerfully. "I was glad to help. Where are you going to have your car towed?"

Um—she dug into her purse again to cover her confusion. "I have no idea. I don't even know if anyone in town repairs Subarus."

"Me, either." He shook his head. "I've only been back the past couple of months. Hopefully you won't have to take it to South Bend."

He swung his door open and jumped out. More slowly, Callie opened hers. The rain had abated, but she hated to lose what warmth she'd gained.

The tow truck rolled up and parked. She tried to think of what to do.

"I can't have it towed home because I don't have a place yet." She gripped her temples. "Right now, I'm staying with the Taylors."

"So I heard. That's outside of town. Do you want Paul to take it there?"

"No, that seems counterproductive—and expensive." *Stop making me think*, her brain cells pleaded. *We're tired. We're chilled.*

"I'm sure you don't want it towed to your aunt and uncle's."

"No way." He remembered them and where they lived? *Oh yeah. Brandy.* Callie gritted her teeth.

She could grow old standing here listing the women Jason had dated.

Jason gently pushed on her back, and they approached the tow truck. "Do Andrea and her parents still attend Eastside?"

"Yes." That protective feeling of his hand again. But what did the church have to do with her stalled car?

"I doubt they'd mind if you left it in their parking lot overnight."

She'd never have thought of that. "Andrea's dad is on their board. If you don't mind talking to Paul about hauling my car out, I'll try to call the Taylors again to see what Rich thinks of the idea. I need to let him and Lana know what's going on."

While Jason and the tow truck owner conferred, her call went through, and a sleepy Rich agreed with the plan. "That will work. You want me to pick you up?"

"Oh no, don't get up." Rich wasn't a night person. "I'll find a way—"

"Tell him I'll bring you home." Jason, deep in a discussion about wet spark plugs and battery connections, pointed to his chest.

He'd been listening? "Well, all right."

She wished she felt as reluctant as she made herself sound. *God, please end this quickly. I don't need to get mixed up emotionally with this man—even if it's only on my side.*

Especially if it's only on my side.

"So you want this towed to Eastside Church?" Paul, big and brawny as his truck, told her the cost. When she confirmed her membership in the AAA Chicago Motor Club, he climbed back into the truck's cab.

"We'll meet you at Eastside." His hand on her back again and more sitting in his car. At sixteen she would have killed to ride in Jason Kenton's car. Now she wondered if she could bear thirty more cramped minutes of inhaling his aftershave and his charm and eau de onion rings.

She didn't have to wait that long. The monster tow truck pulled her little SUV out of the pond as if it were a child's wagon. Jason took a back way to the church, and before she knew it, they'd rendezvoused with Paul at the church parking lot where she'd played hours of Bible school games…prayed with other kids in the church van before leaving for camp… gathered with the youth group to go Christmas caroling. She couldn't wait to go to church tomorrow! Even being with Andrea couldn't compare to the sense of home even the parking lot provided.

"Uh, Callie?"

Paul's truck roared out of the driveway. She realized she'd been standing, staring at the Dumpsters behind the church. "I'm sorry. I was reminiscing."

"We had awesome times here, didn't we?"

We? You showed up for free food and, oh yes, on Graduation Sunday.

"Would you like to reminisce a little more—and dry out— over a cup of coffee?"

She covered her choking noise with a cough. *Do you really want to remember our past?*

Chapter 7

Bring a girl to a root-beer stand for a first date? Um, no. Not even a sort-of date like this.

Jason and his paper-thin billfold loved this retro drive-in, its low prices, and generous burgers that tasted better because of the glowing lights lining its canopy, the neon hamburger-and-shake sign, and the roller-skating carhops. He'd planned to eat here before his escape to South Bend.

But the unthinkable had happened. Callie, fresh from Chicago, shared his car's front seat, sipping coffee because they didn't serve lattes.

He'd tried to suggest Applebee's, but she absolutely refused to set foot even in McD's because of her appearance. He feared she would make him take her home, but he'd managed to sell her on the root-beer stand.

Obviously she thought she resembled a slimy creature that had just crawled from a swamp.

The truth: Her wet black hair had lost its trendy wispy look and now waved softly around her extraordinary face. Weariness and shadows from the drive-in's canopy softened her emerald-sparkly eyes to deep jade. She looked waiflike and vulnerable clutching his oversized jacket around her, and it was all he could do to keep from pulling her to him. Instead, he gripped his burger as if it would run away and tried to think of something brilliant to say.

"Uh, how's your coffee?"

She stirred it. "Hot."

She wasn't doing any better. Or after he'd embarrassed her at the wedding shower, maybe she was wreaking monosyllabic revenge on him. He gulped his drink and tried again. "I've never ordered coffee here. For me, a warm summer night always equals an extra-large frosty mug of root beer."

Especially when he'd run the heater to stop her shivering. It was June, for crying out loud. She couldn't be *that* cold. Still, he held up his mug, as if toasting her.

"Yeah, I like their root beer." She wasn't looking right at him, but he thought he saw a sparkle stray from her eye. "When I thought I'd die from the heat, I walked here from the trailer court, and cold root beer tasted so-o-o good. After band camp—"

"Who could forget that?" He was feeling hotter and hotter. "We marched a gazillion miles on blacktop. It must have been two hundred degrees—"

"Andrea and I came here afterward and held those icy mugs against our cheeks—"

He winced. He wouldn't mind if he never saw Andrea again this side of heaven.

"I'm sorry." Callie looked down at her coffee cup. "I shouldn't have mentioned her, after this evening—"

"I shouldn't have played at her shower in the first place." Why had he thought he could fool Andrea? If only he hadn't played "Think of Me." He'd forgotten how she'd considered it "their" song. *Stupid, stupid, stupid.*

"Your music sounded wonderful, though." Callie sipped as if at a tea party. "I hadn't heard you play in ages."

"Thanks." She'd fixed her eyes on the wooden menu on the side of the little white stand.

How much had Andrea told her? He wished he knew—but not really…. *Lord, I'm messing up big-time, here. What do I say? What do I do?*

The church. They'd stood together at the place where both their faith journeys had begun years before. Perhaps it could connect them now. Jason said, "I'm sorry your car had to be towed. But it was great seeing the church again. Those days in the youth group meant more to me than I realized then."

"Did they?"

Whoa, green fire in those eyes. Maybe reminiscing was a bad idea. Still, he'd spoken the truth. Jason raised his chin. "Yes, they did. I know I didn't act like I heard a word Pastor Dustin said. You tried to tell me, too—"

"Did I ever." Now she winced. "I was the Cowgirl from God. I drew tracts on people like pistols."

He laughed. "You were trying to help me." *You were trying to help Brandy, too, but I won't bring that up.*

"Maybe." She grimaced. "But mostly, I think I liked being right."

An oddly refreshing conversation. Refreshing, but not comfortable.

She crossed her arms. Was she shutting him out? Or trying to hide the fact she still shivered?

He tapped her nearly empty cup. "Would you like a nice, hot refill?"

"That sounds wonderful."

He gestured to a carhop lounging near the stand's door, who skated to his car window as easily as other people walked.

"Could you bring us another coffee, double cream?" He and Callie drank their coffee the same. Incredible—they actually agreed on something?

"Sure." The guy zoomed off and returned with Callie's drink without spilling a drop.

Jason served her with a flourish. "Would you also like to start a new page?"

"Excuse me?"

"Delete the old ones, which seem to be getting us nowhere. Start new ones—as in, 'Hello, how are things going? What's new in your life right now?'"

"All right." Her shoulders visibly relaxed, but her face wore a wary expression.

So the ball was in his court. He told her about graduation from Bethel, his work on his master's degree, and his students. "You are speaking to the most musically accomplished barista Starbucks ever hired."

Her raised eyebrows asked several questions: Didn't you earn a scholarship to Northwestern in Chicago? Why did you graduate five years after I did? Thankfully, she only asked, "So you live in South Bend?"

He stuck to the script. "I did live there until Grandpa had a heart attack in April. My folks live in Texas now, so they couldn't stay to take care of him. I offered to move in and help out until Grandpa's better."

Approval bloomed in her face. He wanted to take out his phone and capture that smile forever. Instead, he said, "They let me stay rent free, so it works out well on my end, too." He grinned. "Plus I'm helping him prepare for the Blueberry Festival. He thinks he's going to do all the stuff he normally does, but Grandma and I know better."

"Sounds like you'll be extra busy this year. Will you have to park cars?"

"I hope not." Like every other teen in sports or clubs, he

and Callie had risked life and limb directing thousands of confused visitors to festival parking. "Actually, I'm hoping to open this year for Dane Dodson and the Great Great Lakes Orchestra. We've been e-mailing and trying to work out the details."

"Really? That would be awesome." Callie seemed to have forgotten her shivers. "When I saw them on *The Next Great American Band*, I kept saying, 'Wow, he grew up in Plymouth. I know him.'"

"I like what he stands for, too," Jason said. "He's given his music and his career to God. I'm trying to do the same."

Her eyes widened, and a smile traveled halfway across her face, then halted, as if unsure of where to go. She said quietly, "I hope it works out for you."

"So do I." He felt like scratching his head. In high school, Callie celebrated when he made occasional efforts to grow closer to God. How many times had he hid in the boys' restroom to escape her praise-the-Lord antics? Now she acted as if he didn't mean it. Or—and this really blew him away—during the past decade, could *she* have walked away from Christ?

He didn't know what to say, so he asked, "When was the last time you went to the festival?"

"At least five years ago." The caution in her face melted into a look of yearning that surprised him.

"You mean to tell me that you haven't bought an authentic Blueberry Festival teddy-bear tissue box cover from the craft tents or watched the Blueberry Stomp or the official arm wrestling match in five whole years?"

"Worse yet." She shook her head in mock tragedian style. "I haven't eaten one of Hort's Heavenly Elephant Ears since 2006."

"I'm surprised you've survived." Despite his concern for her, his mouth watered, just thinking of the golden brown, cinnamon-sugary treat.

"I'll eat my fill this year. It's good to be back."

He leaned forward and lowered his voice. "Why did you come back, Callie? I heard you were taking Chicago by storm. Didn't you like it?"

"I liked lots of things about it." Her face pinked. "I just knew it was time for a change."

She talked about Chicago—Grant Park, Navy Pier, the theaters, the museums, even the positive aspects of her job—maintaining a careful camouflage of anything that might speak of her years of spiritual famine.

She mentioned her new involvement with the church youth, but she didn't want to share her revived passion for their welfare with Jason. She'd let him talk her into coming here, but why should she trust him? He'd always demonstrated a talent for twisting holy issues for his own purpose.

So what if he'd undergone a transformation? Jason experienced numerous "conversions" during high school. When he quoted scripture and led in prayer at youth group, Callie had wanted to shout from the rooftops, "I prayed for him! He's come to Christ!"

Jason's new life often lasted several days—but rarely through the weekend.

Saturday nights, Brandy sauntered in late from her dates with him. Entering the bedroom she shared with Callie, Brandy kicked off her shoes, tossed her bag against the mobile home's wall, and even shook Callie awake. Brandy then shared all the juicy details of her evening.

Now, stuffing those memories in the back of her mental closet, Callie kept up the casual chitchat about her job search. "I hope an offer comes through soon. I'm not sure I can take sharing an office with a cow much longer."

He laughed and laughed when she told him about her temp job. She steered Jason away from any below-the-surface snags that might rip open their conventional so-what-have-you-been-doing conversation.

Still looking for excitement, Mr. Hottie? Miss Blueberry is back. But she's not nearly as naive as she used to be.

Callie slapped her tennis racket at the ball with all her might. An empty *whoosh!* The ball barely hit the line behind her before bouncing into the grass.

"Game. You won!" She said it to preserve her lifelong reputation as a good sport—which, she knew, had always bugged Brandy.

Sure enough, her cousin's mouth tightened, even as she raised her racket in triumph.

Callie gave herself a little shake. *No more mind games, Callie. You came because you cared, right?*

Brandy shouldered her racket. "Let's cool down before we walk home."

The June morning already sizzled. They headed for the nearby shelter house with their water bottles. Still, Callie preferred Centennial Park anytime, compared to her relatives' air-conditioned trailer. She gulped water, wishing she'd skipped her earlier run and wondering why Brandy had invited her to play.

She didn't have to wonder long.

"Come on, Callie. A few hundred dollars? You can afford it." Brandy smiled then downed water from her bottle, though, as usual, her tennis game hadn't made her work up a sweat. How did someone who smoked like a factory look so good after exercise?

Callie, on the other hand, felt drippy, beet red, winded—and caged, though Brandy's tone cajoled her. Why hadn't she seen through Brandy's sudden friendliness? Callie fanned herself with her racket. "You know I'm only working part-time."

Her cousin chuckled—not a very nice chuckle. "You had

enough money to throw Andrea a party out at Swan Lake. Quite the social event, I heard."

"It was Andrea's party, Brandy. Not mine. She wrote the guest list."

"You could have asked her to include me—if you'd wanted."

Actually, no. Andrea wouldn't have shown up if you'd come. Callie sighed. "Why do you need the money?"

"I want to take a Saturday college course at IUSB. Mom makes me kick in for rent, and with my rotten job, I'll never save enough to go to school."

Try saving your cigarette money. Callie struggled to block the never-ending stream of *nyah-nyah* sentences that flowed through her mind whenever she encountered her cousin. *Lord, I want to learn to love Brandy. Why does she make it so hard?* Aloud, she said, "I'm glad you want to go to school. Be sure to check into financial aid—"

"I filled out a stupid application. I may wait forever before it does any good."

Forever? Maybe a month? Two? Still, Callie didn't want to discourage this new direction. "Show me proof you're registered at IUSB—"

"Proof?" Brandy's eyes narrowed into pale slits. "Are you like a lawyer or something? I thought we were family."

"We are family." *Unfortunately.* "But you've had problems in the past, Brandy. So I'll need to see paperwork from IUSB that tells me you're pursuing an education."

"And not buying booze or dope with it, right?" Brandy's whitened smile resembled a snarl.

"Show me proof from IUSB or another college, and I'll pay half of your first course," Callie said. "You might try Bethel, too. They offer good adult courses and special rates."

"No way." Brandy bounced a ball with her racket. "They already messed with Jason. I won't let them mess with me." She wandered to the nearest backstop and slapped the ball against it repeatedly. Her shapely legs leaped under her tennis skirt, and her long black braid swung back and forth while young men in the next court watched her every move.

Bethel messed with Jason? Callie's heart beat faster. If Brandy saw a difference in his lifestyle, maybe he was for real this time. Maybe.

Brandy smacked a final shot, grabbed the ball, and threw her audience a potent good-bye smile before turning to Callie. "Want a cold diet cola? I think there are a couple in the fridge at home."

She sounded so friendly and cousin-like, Callie, who'd felt as if she'd been pushing on an invisible door, almost fell when it opened. "Uh, yeah. That would taste good."

She didn't want to go. But Callie picked up her racket and walked with her cousin back to the trailer court.

Learning to love Brandy would take more than prayer.

Chapter 8

Eastside Community had replaced the orange shag carpet in its sanctuary years before with a neutral blend that didn't show dirt. But Jason discovered the same sunset-hued rug preserved in the basement prayer room, where he'd gone to read the Bible before his Sunday morning concert.

Stringy and only slightly faded, it welcomed him like an old friend. Jason sat on the metal folding chair and bowed his head, thanking the Lord for His faithfulness, the Hound of Heaven way God had pursued him. Jason asked Him to bless his performance so the congregation would praise God and grow closer to Him.

Leaving the prayer room, he ran straight into Callie and Andrea exiting the ladies' room. Callie's eyes widened, accompanied by an unmistakable grin before she subdued it.

"Good morning." He offered his best smile.

Andrea uttered a stiff "Hello."

Callie echoed his greeting. "Thanks again for rescuing me last week."

"I was glad to help."

Callie glanced at her church bulletin. "You're playing this morning?"

"Sure am." He liked the anticipation in her voice. "I'm really looking forward to it."

"I have to meet with the youth committee before service." Andrea steered Callie away.

Flicking a quick wave, she disappeared down a hallway with her disgruntled friend.

Lord, please help me keep my mind on You today. Not on his failings with Andrea. Not on Callie and the surge of more-than-interest that turned his head and heart toward the hallway. *I'm here to worship You. To help others worship You.*

When Reverend Whitaker from Eastside had contacted him about playing, he'd tried to refuse, explaining about his past.

"All the more reason to play for us," the pastor had said. "I know your pastor in South Bend and others who have heard you minister. I talked to a Bethel professor who knows you. You've turned around one hundred eighty degrees. Our people need to see God's power at work."

Jason straightened and started up the steps.

Callie thought Jason had played beautifully at Andrea's shower.

But this is marvelous. Majestic. Magnificent. She ran out of adjectives trying to describe the music pouring from keyboards like living water. Gracious old hymns, upbeat contemporary songs, compelling classical pieces. He wove them into a musical tapestry that made her feel like falling to her knees.

Between songs, Callie glanced sideways at Andrea, unmoving as the little-girl statue in her parents' front yard.

Thank you, Lord, that Patrick's out of town on business. Callie didn't want to imagine that complication.

Andrea had insisted they sit near the back of the church, but Rich and Lana, unaware of their daughter's past relationship with Jason, had won the debate. They all sat a few rows away from the platform—a perfect spot to watch this master pianist offer his art to God.

Jason's strong hands commanded the music, soft and then loud, to come forth. She'd never before seen that joy on his face, innocent as a child's, powerful as a champion's.

She closed her eyes to keep from being distracted, to focus her mind and heart on the worship they shared.

Thank You, Lord, because You forgive and create anew. Thank You for Your grace.

He'd spoken with everyone who approached him—sweet little old ladies wearing polyester pantsuits, middle-aged couples who wanted college recommendations for their teens, adolescent girls who blushed and giggled, little kids who wanted to bang on his keyboard. An exceptional number of people seemed to understand what he was doing. They had worshipped with Jason and wanted to share their appreciation with him.

Pastor Sam slapped him on the back. "See? I told you God would bless this concert."

Jason nodded, gratitude swelling in his chest. "I enjoyed every minute. Your people understand how to worship God through music. You must have taught them well."

After meeting the youth pastor, who took his card and promised to call him about a possible event, Jason finally allowed himself to approach Callie, who was talking with several teens.

He'd thought her lovely at the shower and even after she'd gone swimming under the viaduct. But today, connecting with the kids, her face showed excitement he hadn't seen in her, even as a go-get-'em teenage evangelist. He'd stolen a glance or two at her while he played. Eyes closed, lips moving in silent prayer, she lifted her face to heaven. Whatever struggles Callie had experienced before she returned to Plymouth, she knew God now.

"Hi, Jason."

She'd never greeted him first before. "Hi, Callie."

She turned back to the teens. "Desiree, Austin, Tasha, Brandon, this is Jason Kenton. He used to come to our church a long time ago—"

"You make me sound like a fossil." He grinned.

"Now he's studying and teaching music. Lucky people like us get to listen to him play in concerts."

The look she gave him nearly liquefied his knees. "I—I hope it blessed you."

"Awesome!" The big red-headed kid crushed Jason's hand in his. "I like guitar better than piano music, but I wish I could hear you again."

The short dark-haired girl said, "You made me want to worship Jesus."

Callie nodded. Did he see a tear in her eye?

He choked up himself, and it wasn't just his tie.

He offered his hand, and she took it. His fingers curled around her fragile ones, not wanting to let go. He couldn't afford to take them out to eat today, not even at the root-beer stand. But maybe they could walk around the park before his shift at Starbucks. The teens already had turned to yak with their friends. Callie's eyes met his without blinking, and his mouth went dry. "Would—would you like to—"

"Hurry, Callie, Mom and Dad are going to Applebee's for dinner." Andrea brushed past him.

With Andrea's return, wariness crept over Callie's expressive face again, but it mingled with joy and frustration. She paused so long he dared hope she would fracture the invisible chain Andrea tugged.

"Come on." Andrea touched her other arm.

"All right." Callie edged away from her. "I'll come in a sec."

Reluctantly, he released her hand.

"Thanks again for an incredible worship experience." Her dazzling smile almost blinded him, and he forgot to ask for her cell number. She walked away.

Slowly he returned to the sanctuary to collect his stuff. When the big red-headed kid spotted Jason dismantling his keyboard, he and a couple of other teens offered to help load up. Austin asked him a hundred questions about the life of a professional musician. His friendliness lightened Jason's loneliness. By the time he knocked knuckles with the teens and honked as he left Eastside's parking lot, he'd made a decision. One he'd been putting off.

His performance and Starbucks schedules had always messed with regular church attendance, but his move to Plymouth really had thrown in a wrench. He loved his South Bend church and would maintain connections there, but while he lived here, he wanted to worship with this special congregation, with the teens—and especially with Callie.

He recalled Callie's dark head following her best bud out the church door. He had to get to know her better.

Would Andrea let him?

Chapter 9

"May I speak to Callie Creighton, please?" The nasal voice crackled in her cell.

"Speaking." Was this the call she'd waited for? Callie pushed aside the remnants of Lana's pecan pancakes. *Lord, please let it be so.*

"This is Amy Ross of the Notre Dame Office of Public Affairs and Communications. We would like to interview you within the next few weeks for a position in our department."

Discussing dates and times, Callie kept her voice professional, though she wanted to dance on the Taylors' dining room table. She'd hoped for an interview with her alma mater. After playing part-time cowsitter with Cocoa, an interview for a real job! This one, involving media, public speaking, and research, sounded ideal.

When she hung up, Lana poked her head out the kitchen door, wearing a smile that matched Callie's. "Was that what I think it was?"

"Yesss!" Callie pumped her fist. "An interview with Notre Dame!"

"Hurrah!" Lana, though small as Andrea, gave Callie a bear hug that left her breathless—and reminded her of her mother's hugs. Three-second videos of Mom's face played in her mind: Mom exclaiming about her first-grade papers; Mom's pink-lipsticked mouth puckered to help Callie blow out birthday candles. Even as tears threatened to escape her eyes, she reveled in the warmth of Lana's arms. What would she have done without the Taylors?

Callie's interview prospect made the chaos of her six-kid afternoon at the dairy bearable. When she met Andrea in the driveway after work, Callie told her the good news. Together they squealed and boogied into the house like middle schoolers.

"I told you so," Andrea gasped, falling into a chair on the Taylors' enormous front porch. "I knew the perfect job would show up soon."

"It's an interview, not a job," Callie reminded her. "This probably is just the first round. At least, it's something." Though she wouldn't go back to Chicago, its enormous job market certainly had presented more opportunities than those in Indiana's smaller cities. "I've felt downright lazy lately." *And more than a little scared.*

"Yeah, right," Andrea snorted. "You *are* working, remember?"

"Part time." Callie shrugged. She couldn't escape the tinge of fear that nagged her as if she were destitute. *A leftover from my trailer court days, I guess.*

"You spend hours at the computer researching wedding stuff for me. You do errands when I can't—"

"You've helped me get ready for the wedding, too. Actually, I'm not sure I want you to get a full-time job." Lana grinned. "You'll move out on me."

"Yeah, you and Mom and your cleaning fetish." Andrea tsk-tsked at her. "Callie, you're so-o-o lazy."

"Notre Dame scheduled this interview for August 10th, so I'm still at your service for at least another couple of weeks." Callie consulted her phone. "Unless, of course, interview requests start rolling in by the dozen."

To her surprise, more did. Not by the dozen, but she enjoyed seeing appointments on her calendar again—appointments other than Aunt Sheila and Uncle Alan.

Still, she visited them weekly. A few days later, on a surprisingly cool July day, she coaxed her relatives onto their deck.

Desiree and Tasha walked past and waved at Callie, warming her heart. "See you at youth group!" she called.

"Who's that?" Aunt Sheila touched up a nail with bright orange polish.

"Kids from my church."

Uncle Alan grunted. Aunt Sheila said nothing and touched up another nail.

Callie decided not to elaborate. As usual, they'd run out of safe conversation topics. Brandy certainly wasn't a relaxing one. Still, Callie needed to ask about her absent cousin. She kept her tone casual. "How's Brandy?"

"Hardly ever see her." Uncle Alan, resting a beer on his potbelly, stretched his white, skinny legs across the deck. "Just as well."

Callie tried not to echo the thought. After Brandy had shown her an IUSB registration slip, she'd written Brandy a check. Immediately her cousin disappeared, never returning Callie's calls.

"When she shows up, she don't talk much." Lines of worry furrowed Aunt Sheila's forehead like garden rows.

"I'm praying for her." Callie touched her shoulder.

Her aunt looked a little skeptical, but touched Callie's hand. "Well, thank you."

"It'll take a lot more than prayin' to change that girl." Uncle Alan sucked in another king-sized gulp.

Her? How about you? Callie couldn't offer money to Aunt Sheila because her husband would only drink it up.

Her aunt must have felt her frustration because, when Callie rose to leave, she gave her a rare hug. "Thanks for the pretty geranium, hon, and the groceries."

"You're welcome." *I do love you, Aunt Sheila. I appreciate your taking me in after Dad died. But you all need Jesus. I wish you'd let me introduce you to Him.*

That evening, as Callie and Andrea rode to church, Callie dumped her concerns about them on her friend.

"Your aunt and uncle took care of you—kind of—so it's right to care about them." Andrea gave her a look of admiration. "But I don't know how you can stand it."

"I can't. Especially when Uncle Alan's conscious. If there were an award for Worst-Looking Man in Shorts, he'd win, hands down." Callie shuddered. "I might have hit the booze hard, too, if you and Jesus hadn't rescued me."

"You're different. You were my best friend from the first time I saw you." Andrea turned into Eastside's parking lot. "I'm so glad you're back. So happy you want to help us with the youth group."

One part of Callie listened with joy. Another part jolted with the discovery of a familiar shabby blue Mazda parked a few spaces away.

Her heart choked and sputtered like Jason's car. What was he doing here?

"What is *he* doing here?" Andrea's whisper, upon spotting Jason in the church foyer, carried an entirely different tone.

Laughing and talking with Austin, Jason looked comfortable and at ease. Did he see her yet? Callie tried not to stare.

His warm glance searched, touched, rested on her, melting her like gelato in July. *Oh yeah. He sees me.*

Pastor Eric solved the mystery after they all trouped into the purple-walled youth room. "Welcome, everyone. Great to see you." Teens dropped into comfortable castoff chairs and sofas while others found seats on the floor. "We're especially glad to have Callie and Jason here. Callie's agreed to help us out for a while, and Jason's going to share his testimony with us tonight."

Callie and Jason. Reddening, she fought the idea that their names sounded nice together.

Clapping and *woots* erupted from Austin and his friends. Girls' dreamy gazes fastened on Jason. Callie, not daring to look at Andrea, smiled at Austin, at Desiree, at Tasha, at anyone but Jason.

His eyes, brown-sugar delicious, met hers again. Callie tried to pull away, but knew she was gawking and blushing like an adolescent.

She felt Andrea's silence, heavy as a boulder, beside her.

Pastor Eric was praying. With a sense of relief, she bowed her head, disconnecting the eye contact between Jason and her. She tried to yank her thoughts back and make them act like they were in church. *What about Jason?* they yammered. *What will* you *do?*

Callie had been talking to Desiree, gesturing with her hands in that awkward yet feminine way she had, and he hardly saw anything else. Now, when Eric announced they were going to pray, Jason gratefully closed his eyes. Prayer always brought him focus, helped him remember why he came to church.

The teens' young voices, lifted in concern for their families and friends, moved him to pray silently for his own. For his parents, grateful for his change of lifestyle but clueless as to why he had changed. For his tired grandma. For Grandpa, who tried to hide his fear of dying in orneriness. For his old band friend, Trevor, running at top speed toward a cliff he didn't see.

Prayer readied him for worship. A girl at the keyboard struck the opening chords to the first song. Eric played a mean electric guitar. The high school kid who banged the drums kept a decent beat. This bunch really sang well. A couple of excellent voices led out—one was Austin's—but their enthusiasm surpassed the excellence. The words of praise reflected in their faces. Old hymns, pounding contemporary songs—their fervor didn't change. By the end of the worship time, he felt they had ministered to him more than he would to them.

Now came the tough part.

Eric had asked him to briefly share how Christ had changed his life. As a teen, Jason did that after church camp; again, after a big Jesus concert; and again, after a famous Christian athlete came to town. He liked the way it put him on center stage, at least for a few days. Church people practically threw confetti when you said you'd been converted or rededicated your life.

Now when Eric introduced him, he stood before the group feeling like a hypocrite—especially with Andrea glaring at him.

Jason straightened and raised his head. "Hey, did you know I went to church here when I was a teen?"

Maybe he shouldn't have started that way. The kids didn't look exactly overwhelmed. Callie cocked her head, an "Oh yeah?" look on her face.

"I learned the right things to say, even the right songs. I didn't mean them. Because if you really mean something, you live it. I hurt myself, and I hurt a lot of other people. Still, Jesus didn't give up on me."

He told them how he'd partied and flunked out of college twice, and that his parents finally told him they wouldn't support him anymore.

"I wanted to be a rock star and thought the friends I played with in my band would support me." He snorted. "My habits hurt my music, my ability to perform. My buds didn't want me mooching off them, either."

He finally came home and decided to change. "I enrolled at Bethel College because my mom's cousin turned his life around there. Mom talked my dad into forking out tuition for the first semester. Besides, Bethel was the only school that would give me a chance. My roommate, Elijah, a crazy guy who cared, finally convinced me God wanted to forgive me and help me put my life back together. I don't know what He has in store for me now. I know He'll never give up on me."

"And He'll never give up on you."

He sat at the keyboard and began to sing "Amazing Grace."

"You really believe Jason, don't you?" Andrea, wearing a terry cloth robe and jerking a brush through her hair, glowered at her oval bedroom mirror. The heat of her antagonism radiated back to Callie so she almost felt sunburned.

"Yes, I do." Callie, sitting on Andrea's antique bed, tried not to wince—or disturb the perfect arrangement of Andrea's nine pillows on the down quilt.

"I can't believe you're falling for that old line. Don't you remember in high school—"

"Of course I remember. But people can change." Callie crossed her arms.

"He can't." Andrea almost threw her brush into a drawer and rose to slam it shut.

"Of course he can't. Neither can I, not without God's help." Callie stood beside her friend. "Are you saying God can't change him?"

Andrea faced Callie and fastened earnest eyes on her. "I'm not saying that at all. I'm saying this is an act." Her face flushed, but she didn't turn away. "When Jason first came on to me, he used a spiritual approach. For the first time in his life, things weren't going his way. He and his family were feuding, and he felt alone. He needed a friend to point him to God."

She dropped her chin. "Though fighting for my own spiritual life, I didn't realize I needed help, too. I thought I was strong. I'd always helped others. Of course I could help Jason. I was wrong."

Callie slipped her arms around her friend. Anger at the old Jason simmered. How could he have used Andrea—and so many others—that way? Yet his words during youth group rang with authenticity. He had not excused his sin. He had warned the kids against following the same destructive path.

Andrea stepped back and looked her in the face. "Besides Patrick, you're the only person in the world I've told about Jason. Even when Pastor Sam counseled me, I told him I'd been involved with a guy, but I didn't give his name." Her eyes hardened into blue steel. "I could hardly sit there tonight among all those starry-eyed girls in our youth group, listening to him—"

"What will you do? Chase him away from Eastside? Post armed guards?" Callie knew her friend made valid points, but she could not erase mental pictures of Jason praying, worshipping, speaking to the kids with love and concern in his voice. "Isn't the church supposed to welcome sinners, as Jesus did?"

"You sound just like I did," Andrea groaned and dropped onto the bed.

"Jesus welcomed me back. I can't forget that." Callie sat beside her, softening her voice. "I know you're telling me this because you care about me. I understand your concern about the youth group. Talk to the pastors if you think that's necessary. All I'm saying is give Jason a chance. Let God work in his life, through his life."

"I could do it better if he lived on the moon," Andrea grumbled. "And if he didn't have his eyes on you. If he insists on hanging around, I'm going to watch him like a hawk."

"I'm sure he knows that." Callie tried not to grin. Andrea, despite her little-girl face and long, wavy hair, looked scary as a samurai. "Come on. Let's change the subject. Let's talk about how gorgeous you're going to look in your wedding gown one month from now."

She pulled the enormous dress bag from the closet and opened it, watching the cloud of fragile silk and lace work its usual magic.

"I'd much rather think about Patrick." Andrea's tight mouth relaxed into a small smile. She ran her fingers along the tiny, intricate tucks in her dress's bodice. Callie helped her shift its full ruffled skirt so Andrea could hold it up to admire in the mirror.

They lapsed into girl talk about manicures, pedicures, and whether Andrea should wear her hair up or down.

Later Callie lay wide awake in the guest room next door, breathing the faint fragrance of lavender from embroidered sheets, remembering Jason's intensity at church, his kindness in helping fish her car out of the viaduct flood, his boyish grin from behind the plants at the shower. Ooh, he had never looked more handsome than on that night—wonderful hair, wonderful eyes, almost perfect music…if only Andrea hadn't detected his presence.

Callie sighed. She should have known better. Andrea missed nothing. Her forceful words echoed in Callie's head: *"I'm going to watch him like a hawk."*

Uneasiness nibbled at the peaceful night with sharp little teeth. Surely her friend no longer harbored feelings for Jason? Ridiculous. Callie recalled Andrea's expression as she spoke of Patrick and caressed her wedding dress.

Why couldn't she put the past behind her and forgive? Why did Andrea focus on Jason with such fierce feeling?

Callie shifted from her side to her back, then clasped her hands behind her head, then punched her pillow and shifted to her side again. She was letting her imagination run away with her. Andrea was her forever friend, and she was playing dragon lady because she didn't want Callie to be hurt. But the thought was hardly reassuring.

Does she think she's going to watch me, too?

Chapter 10

Jason should have known serving the Eastside youth would begin with a blast of ketchup.

He'd shared and performed at enough youth events to know the lengths to which youth pastors would go to break the ice, break up cliques, and bring their kids together in crazy competitions.

Plus Pastor Eric, after shaking Jason's hand and accepting his offer to help, told him to wear old jeans and a T-shirt to the next meeting.

Tonight Eric had supplied each and every teen with a squeeze bottle of ketchup, mustard, or green gunk that defied identity. Now, standing on a chair in the parking lot, the youth pastor gave an earsplitting whistle that quieted the mob's bloodthirsty roar to a mutter. He read the rules of the gross game.

I don't have a good feeling about this. Jason understood

the function of games in youth ministry, but even as a teen, he'd never cared for getting down and dirty.

Eric pointed to Jason. "You guys can attack him or me any-where out in the field behind the church."

Jason didn't remember volunteering for this.

"Mr. Anthony gave us permission to run through his woods, too. But don't go beyond his fence. Stay out of the parking lot and *don't* enter the church without permission."

He gestured to Jason. "Come on, man. We get a thirty-second head start."

They took off as if trying to set new Olympic records. The horde soon followed, and Jason sprinted for his life. Good thing he'd been running a few times a week, or he quickly would have joined the roll of martyrs for the faith.

Callie helped out at a supply station in the field. She mostly laughed at him every time he dashed past, but once she whipped out a bottle of ketchup and managed to squirt him on the back of his neck. He felt the goo inch down his back.

Thankfully the game soon ended, and he looked forward to washing up. The shot Callie took at him proved the most damaging—how could he clean all that stuff off without tak-ing a shower?

No problem. The youth group helped by blasting him and their pastor with a hose. He still ended up smelling like a dou-ble cheeseburger. Not so bad for helping out a youth group.

Not so good if you wanted to ask a girl out.

Scrubbing his hair with a towel, Jason shook his head at his reflection in the church restroom mirror. Could he wait another day to ask her? Should he?

He really didn't want to.

After his first impulsive near invite at his Sunday morning concert, he'd prayed more and thought things through. First, he believed he should worship and serve the teens at Eastside. Second, he wanted to watch Callie in action.

When he finally returned to the youth room, she was circulating among the kids, talking and laughing. He'd heard Eric say Callie had been helping out only a couple of weeks, but she acted as if she'd always served here. Perhaps one more piece of evidence that she did not ever intend to return to Chicago?

Kidding with Austin and his friends, Jason cast several glances her way. Despite her trendy hair and clothes, few would have guessed a few short weeks ago Callie worked for a high-powered advertising firm in Chicago. She poured lemonade, cleaned up spills, and popped more popcorn. He admired her knack for drawing out the quiet kids.

Before he realized he was staring at her, Andrea's radar found him. She leveled a scowl at Jason as she gathered her prayer group. He returned a smile. God had forgiven him, even if she hadn't. *Lord, please don't let her intimidate Callie.*

Sitting beside Eric in his guys' prayer group, Jason let God's Spirit focus him on the boys' requests. Afterward, Eric taught an excellent Bible study. Callie commented once and asked a question that blew Jason out of the water. No one could do that without considerable study and thought.

Ketchup or no ketchup, he wanted to be with a girl like that.

So after most of the kids left, Andrea counseled a girl in another room, and he and Callie swept up popcorn. Jason said, "It's a perfect night for a walk in the park. You want to get some exercise with me?"

Callie straightened, an odd expression in those amazing eyes. She fumbled with a bracelet on her arm, saying nothing.

Had he read her wrong? Or had Andrea scared her away from him? Sweat broke out on his palms. He'd never been turned down before.

Finally a weird little smile crinkled her lips. "All right. I'll go tell Andrea, since I rode with her."

What was going through her mind? He had no idea, but she'd said yes. His whole body breathed a sigh of relief. Right now, that was enough.

"Glorious. Glorious! I love seeing the whole sky." Callie, her arms open wide, had whirled in a little-girl circle before she realized it.

Jason, walking beside her alongside the tennis courts, grinned. "I guess I don't think of it that way. It's not like Plymouth is close to the ocean or mountains or anything."

"I can't tell you what it feels like to see more than a little piece of a sunset." She waved her hand at the rose, violet, and gold canvas spreading across the deep blue heavens above them. "Living near downtown Chicago, it's as if a Monet masterpiece were covered with only a corner showing. It made me crazy, especially when I knew God was painting a new picture every day."

He blinked. "What about Lake Michigan?"

"Well, yeah." She wasn't explaining this very well. "I loved running or skating along the shoreline, especially early in the morning. Still, Grant Park was always crowded, and I never escaped the traffic sounds so I could just sit and think. Still I felt alone."

"Hey, it hasn't been that long since I lived in South Bend." The famous Jason smile teased her, yet his eyes looked serious. "I know what you mean. You didn't feel at home."

He understood. He really did. This trickle of closeness between them made her wish for a flood. But it also made her want to build a wall.

She said, "Andrea's wedding brought me back to Plymouth. When I drove past the city limits sign, though, I felt I'd come home to stay."

Centennial Park's covered bridge loomed before them.

Jason said, "When I was a little guy, I dashed through the bridge as fast as I could because I was scared of the dark."

Callie shook her head. "I hardly believe that. Even in kindergarten, you seemed so self-assured."

"You mean obnoxious?" He grinned.

"Well…" She let her eyes twinkle, but as their feet thudded into the cool, shadowy depths of the bridge, she changed the subject. "It's hard to believe in a few short weeks this bridge will be so jammed I could raise my feet and let the crowd carry me to the other side."

"Yeah, half a million people coming to town kind of changes things. Changes things at Grandpa's, too." Jason chuckled. "The Blueberry Festival is his whole world. He heads up transportation, and I'm trying to keep him from killing himself. I help him, and a committee carries part of the burden, but I know he lies awake at night. He's always working out better ways to take visitors from parking lots to the festival."

"Are you going to drive a tram?" As a child, Callie thought the long shaded wagonloads of passengers resembled giant caterpillars. She hadn't dreamed of becoming Miss Blueberry. Instead, she'd longed to bounce on the seat of one of the tractors that pulled trams, waving to everyone along the way.

"Not sure Grandpa will trust me." Jason brought her back to the present. "I smashed up several cars when I was a teen. He can't seem to understand that was ten years ago."

The darkness of the bridge's interior kept her from seeing Jason's face. But she heard the tension in his voice.

Time to change the subject again. "Did Dane and the Great Great Lakes Orchestra work out?"

His tone brightened. "In his last e-mail, he sounded positive and said he would let me know soon. It won't be a big deal, just playing a piece or two before their performance. Connecting with Dane even in a minor way won't hurt in getting new gigs."

His hand touched Callie's, and celebration flowed from him in a warm, joyous current so strong that she drew back.

He didn't seem to notice. "I love teaching, but I guess my real passion is performance. What I wouldn't give to play either solo or in a good band every weekend."

This is the guy who's so big on feeling at home? Why did that stick in her mind like a tiny splinter?

"Although it's really hard to make a living doing it."

The splinter wedged in deeper.

She relaxed when he talked about teaching. As they exited the bridge, she told him about her interviews, but they talked more about the youth group.

"Some kids come from the trailer park, as I did." She shook her head, sadness tightening her throat. "Few of them will ever have friends like the Taylors to take them under their wing."

"How about you?" Jason's eyes reflected the last rays of the sunset. He stopped and gave her a keen look. "You're wonderful with those girls."

After all my screwups? "I'm glad to help, but I'm not the one to mentor them."

"Why not?" The darkness couldn't hide the glow in his eyes.

"I'm really just finding my own way back to God." She bit her lip. "I'm not ready to be a role model—"

"In case you haven't noticed, I haven't passed my perfection test yet. Still, God is talking to me about those kids. When do you think you'll be ready?"

"Um—"

"Never? That's what you're thinking, right?"

I didn't give you permission to read my mind.

"Why don't you pray about it? I'll pray, too."

She'd never gone out with a man who said he'd pray for her. "Okay. I'll pray about it. Still, I think we both need time to grow up, for our sake and for the kids'."

"Maybe you're right. But I'm learning never to underestimate God." He grabbed her hand. This time she didn't pull away.

"Speaking of growing up, we don't always have to act like adults." He tugged her toward the playground. "I won't preach at you anymore. Want to swing?"

She stared at him. Obviously, Jason didn't remember that night years before.

"You're looking at me funny again." He stared back. "Like earlier, when I asked you to go for a walk. Is something wrong?"

"Oh no." Carefully she withdrew her hand.

"Okay, what did I do?" Jason sounded resigned. "I did so many dumb things when I was a kid, I think I'll be apologizing until I'm on social security. If I've offended you—past, present, or future—I really want to say I'm sorry."

"Well…"

"Tell me." He took both her hands.

"It was a teen thing." Callie tried to laugh. "We were sophomores. After youth group one night, you totally amazed me by asking me to walk with you here in the park. *Me*. The girl voted Most Likely to Be Mistaken for a Light Pole. The one who handed you tracts between classes." She shook her head. "I knew you and Brandy had broken up, but I couldn't believe it. Jason Kenton asked me out."

"Okay, I remember now. I guess we spent part of the evening on these swings."

"It was fun. Magical." Remembering, she smiled—for a moment. "Afterward we found a nice, isolated bench under the trees, and you kissed me again and again. I was sweet-sixteen-and-never-been-kissed. For one night, I felt beautiful."

He said nothing for a moment then cocked his head. "Uh, I don't remember things getting out of hand."

"They didn't." She'd gone to bed feeling joyous and a little guilty because super-saints didn't hide on park benches and kiss on a first date. She asked God to forgive her and make her a good influence on her new boyfriend. "But at school the next day, I heard *the* hot story of the hour—you told your buds you went all the way with Fish Face."

"Fish Face?" His jaw dropped. "Oh, Callie. I'm so sorry."

"A junior high nickname shouldn't bother me now." She pulled away.

"It was a stupid nickname. And just one of the stupid, stupid lies I told other guys to make myself feel macho." He groaned. "I was such a fool then."

"I let it get to me far too much." She dug her toe into the ground, inhaling the summer fragrance of freshly cut grass. "Especially since I'm sure nobody believed it."

Brandy hadn't. In fact, she'd laughed at the idea.

Callie closed her eyes. "I always did take things too seriously—"

"No, I don't think so. Callie, would you look at me, please?"

Her chin felt heavy, but she managed to raise it. The streetlight silhouetted him, shining on his perfect hair.

"I'm so, so sorry I hurt you. I hope you can find it in your heart to forgive me." He held out his hand. "Give me a second chance?"

Part of her wanted to walk away and give him a small, stinging sample of what it felt like to be rejected.

Part of her wanted to throw her arms around him and find a bench.

"All right." Slowly, she took his hand. "Only if you give me ten pushes, and I get to choose which swing I want."

His smile lit the night. "I'll give you twenty, if you like. Or thirty. Or a hundred."

"Ten will do." She plopped onto the third swing in the row, the one just the perfect height for her. "I don't want to orbit the moon."

She nearly did. By the fifth push, she told Jason thank you very much, that was enough. He slid onto the swing next to her, and together they rocketed into the sky.

"Bet you can't stand up and swing." With one quick movement, he rose—balancing himself—then pumped up and down with his knees.

"Don't you remember? I could swing higher than any other second grader at Jefferson Elementary, even the boys." She grabbed the chains and lifted herself. Her chest muscles complained. *Ooh, it's been a while.* Ignoring them, she pulled herself to her feet and swung alongside him.

Before long, he dropped to his seat. "We're both going to go flying and break our legs if we don't behave. I'd rather not end this night at the ER."

Laughing, she followed suit. "Mrs. Tindley would have a fit if she saw us."

"Mrs. Tindley? I haven't thought of her in years."

She heard the grimace in his voice. "I think I've repressed how many times during third grade she dragged me down to the principal's office."

"*Nyah-nyah-nyah-nyah-nyah.* I was smart enough to stay out of trouble."

"Yes, you were."

Stretching her legs to their full length, she pointed her toes and soared high into the lovely night. God had outdone Himself, scattering glittering star-sequins throughout the velvet sky. Words rose to her lips that she had to say. "When I consider your heavens, the work of your fingers, the moon and the stars, which you have set in place—"

"What is mankind that you are mindful of them, human beings that you care for them?" Jason finished.

Her heart leaped higher than their swings. "I don't remember quoting Bible verses with you the last time we swung."

"I've learned a few things since then."

They swung awhile in silence, Callie wondering if the scent of lavender in embroidered sheets would awaken her from this fantasy. The thought reminded her of Andrea. She'd covered nicely when Callie told her she was leaving with Jason—but only because of her teen counselee. What would she say when Jason brought her home?

You're my best friend, Andrea. Not my caretaker.

Nevertheless, with a vision of Andrea's face, prolonged swinging, and this evening's burrito supper, her stomach began to protest. She slowed down.

"Want to check out the teeter-totter?" Jason slowed with her.

"Um, no thanks."

"Fine with me." He stopped, reached for her hand, and helped her out of the swing.

Callie couldn't explain why it felt like a courtly gesture. *Jason, you're very, very good at this.* Unease wobbled through her stomach again, especially as she thought of her own past. Jason had spoken honestly at the youth meeting about his failings. She hadn't even hinted to him about Ty.

Why should she? This was their first adult nonemergency-situation date.

The next hour or two with Jason—she lost track, really—dissolved her misgivings. Hand in hand they walked awhile, then crossed the street to a pizza place, where they bought drinks and a personal pan pizza, since she wasn't hungry. They returned through the old stone arch entrance. As a little girl, she'd dreamed of walking through that arch wearing a wedding dress and veil….

Jason led the way to a picnic table not far off the road with a spectacular view of the moon. The night breeze cooled Callie's hot cheeks. She nibbled a sliver of pizza. He ate the rest, and they talked about Ecclesiastes, chapter three, Pastor Eric's subject that night.

She'd never gone on a date like this, full of wisdom, topped with extra cheese and black olives (Jason liked them, too!). Her stomach had settled nicely, and she wanted the evening to last forever.

Unfortunately, she'd lined up an interview, and he'd scheduled an early lesson the next morning in South Bend. So at last they rose from the picnic table. Even the trash can under the moonlit filigree leaves of a tall locust tree seemed beautiful.

What now? As they pitched their trash, she commanded her adolescent heart to walk, not run. But in the soft glow of the night, as Jason turned big, melting eyes on her and took her hands, it struggled to escape.

"Callie…"

"I—I—" She couldn't say what she should.

He dropped her hands gently, but didn't move his gaze. "I would love to kiss you."

I would love that, too. She forced herself not to lean toward him.

"But I want this night to end differently from that night ten years ago."

They didn't touch, yet she felt an almost tangible flow of tenderness between them.

"Callie, do you understand that I want more than just one evening with you?"

"I want to know you better, too." Joy burst in her like fireworks, yet she yearned to hold him. She took a step back. "Let's take our time. No kissing for a while? Nothing that would push us beyond what God wants for us."

"Agreed. For now, nothing closer than holding hands." He gestured toward the parking lot. "I'd probably better take you home before we change our minds."

Chapter 11

Callie dreaded interviewing. She'd stuttered through the first out-of-college ordeals, and several months passed before her polished technique led to the position with Mr. Stonewell.

Today, however, Callie left the public relations office of Harper-Tarrington Industries with that I-aced-it feeling that made her want to dance in the parking lot. If things worked out as she hoped, soon she'd have a job. Her own apartment, where she could come and go on her timetable. The school loan elephant would have to take a hike.

As she inserted her key into the SUV's ignition, her cell rang. *Andrea.* She made a face. "Hi. How's your day going?"

"Wonder of wonders, I'm free for lunch." Her friend's voice sounded too casual. "Want to go to the Dairy Queen?"

"What's the occasion?" They'd lived on chili dogs and ice cream sandwiches as kids, but in readying for her wedding, Andrea had grown paranoid about adding an ounce to her short frame.

"Nothing special. Just wanted to share onion rings with you. I'll even buy you a large hot fudge sundae."

Andrea's ticked about my date with Jason, and she wants to buy me a sundae? "I feel more like a Carolina salad. Let's go to Granny's."

"Okay. Don't ever say I didn't offer you ice cream." Andrea hung up.

Driving away from Plymouth's industrial park, Callie mused about her friend's odd invitation. When Callie slipped into the Taylors' house the night before, still glowing from her walk with Jason, she half expected Andrea to be waiting at the front door with her brother's old BB gun. Callie wasn't sure whom Andrea would shoot first, Jason or herself. However, only the night-light in the foyer greeted her.

Now, entering downtown, she wondered how she'd deal with her unreasonable friend. Andrea needed to see things realistically. *I know Jason has a past, Lord. So have I!*

She pulled up to Granny's. Andrea waved through the glass door.

No weapon that I can see. Callie entered and approached the counter. Granny, a smiling woman with eyes to match, reached over and gave her a hug. "Well, stranger, it's been awhile. Still like Carolina salads?"

"You bet." Callie returned the hug.

"I've already ordered mine." Andrea pointed to a corner booth.

"Be there in a sec."

After Granny took Callie's order they chatted, but an influx of customers cut their reminiscing short. Callie carried her drink to Andrea's table.

"Lunch takes longer here than it did in Chicago." She sat opposite Andrea.

"Always run into a few people I know. At times I don't even

make it through a sandwich." Andrea smiled and sipped her iced tea. "I've extra time today, so we don't have to hurry."

I'd rather hurry. Callie searched her friend's face. She wasn't baring her teeth, and no evil eye contradicted the smile.

"How did the interview go?" Andrea leaned forward.

"Better than I expected. I liked what I saw, and they already set up a second interview with me."

"I'm not surprised. They know a good thing when they see it."

Callie hadn't expected their conversation to start with a compliment. She drew a deep breath. "About last night—"

Andrea only arched her beautifully groomed eyebrows. No eye rolls. No caustic comments. Any more niceness and Callie might explode. "I'm sure you disagree with my going out with Jason."

"I do." Andrea squeezed more lemon into her tea. "After I took Tasha home, I wanted to send out a search party for you. Instead, I decided to pray about it."

"Pray about it?" Callie felt joy, relief—and a twinge of absurd disappointment. She realized she rather enjoyed annoying Andrea.

"Yes, pray. I sat in the youth room and argued with God. A waste of time, of course. Eventually I had to turn you and Jason over to Him. I can't handle either of you. But He can." Smiling, Andrea asked the waitress who'd brought their salads for extra diet honey mustard dressing.

Suspicion coiled inside Callie, ready to spring. "So you're not going to hassle me when we go out again?"

"Nope." Andrea opened her package of crackers without spilling a crumb. "I've warned you as best I can. You're an intelligent Christian woman, and I believe that when Jason comes at you with those big brown eyes, murmuring sweet nothings and quoting Bible verses, you'll see through it. But I'll be praying for you—and even for him."

Quoting Bible verses? Inwardly Callie couldn't help cringing. Andrea looked so calm, so in control that Callie wanted to stuff her salad down her collar. "Will you put us on the church prayer chain? Hold candlelight vigils?"

"Only if you get engaged before Blueberry." Andrea forked a dainty portion of chicken and sugar-roasted pecans into her mouth.

How do I get mad at someone because she's praying for me? Callie attacked her salad, crunching the homemade garlic croutons first.

Andrea nibbled. Callie ground her teeth into lettuce and tomatoes.

Finally she said, "I don't plan to jump into any serious relationship without thought and prayer, Andrea. Do you think I learned nothing from Ty?"

She and Jason had shared their hearts throughout their evening together. So different from her ex.

Andrea shook her head. "You might be on the rebound—"

"Ty and I broke up a year ago. I've already had rebound dates. Jason is different."

Andrea's eyes said, "Different isn't quite how I'd describe him."

"He didn't even kiss me good night." Callie hadn't meant to tell her that, but perhaps now her friend might understand Jason's change was for real.

"He didn't kiss me on our first date, either," Andrea gave her a rueful smile. "Jason is smart. He knows women and how to manipulate them."

Callie could hardly contain her outrage. For a moment they both ignored their Carolina salads and glared at each other.

What is the matter with us? Tears welled up in Callie's eyes. How could she and Andrea be so at odds? She took a deep breath and said, "I think you're living in the past. I really believe he's changed."

Andrea took a deep breath, too. She slid her hand across the table and said quietly, "I hope you're right, Callie. Because you're my best friend, and I want the very best for you."

The boiling tears in Callie's eyes cooled, soothing rather than scalding her. "I know you do."

She reached across the table and locked her pinky finger with Andrea's.

"I think," Andrea said solemnly, "that we need one of Granny's cookies. I'll run off the calories with Patrick tonight." She and her groom-to-be were training for the Blueberry Stomp.

"A cookie apiece," Callie agreed. "Because you'll want oatmeal with macadamia nuts. I want the chocoholic one with the to-die-for icing."

Andrea's smile tinged with sadness. "You'll never learn what's best for you, will you?"

"Maybe as far as cookies go." Callie looked her in the eye. "But as for guys—I think I already know."

Jason thought a short run along Plymouth's Greenway Trail would provide a healthy start to his day.

When he encountered Brandy running in a scanty black-and-green outfit, he felt otherwise.

"Hey, Jason. How's it going?"

Great. Until you showed up. "I might beat a snail."

He'd avoided her since returning to Plymouth. Jason kept running.

Meeting him, she turned and began running alongside. He flinched as she jogged at his elbow.

"Are you going to run the Stomp?"

"Not this year." The 15K Blueberry Stomp hadn't entered his thoughts. "I haven't run that much."

"Maybe you need a running partner." Her long, leopard-like strides pulled his eyes sideways.

He yanked them back to the path ahead. *Give it up, Brandy. We're history.*

He didn't want to blow her off. He didn't want to be rude. Unfortunately, many people in Plymouth still saw Brandy and him as a pair. What if the town grapevine informed Callie he'd been seen with her cousin?

He forged ahead of Brandy as they ran through the woods along Yellow River terrain. She didn't take the hint. The effort winded him so he had to walk when they reached the more public trail near Riverside School.

Brandy, breathing hard, surged to walk beside him. Tossing her long braid, she batted her eyelashes at him, full lips in a pout. "That wasn't very nice."

The woman could flirt if she were lying on her deathbed. *Lord, guide my words. And my thoughts.* Aloud he said, "Sorry we're not in sync, Brandy. I don't think running together would work."

"Oh, I don't know about that." Her smoky sage-colored eyes raked him up and down. "You used to run with me all the time. We were good together."

"Things have changed," he said firmly.

He turned and walked away.

The balloon man at Plymouth's farmer's market twisted skinny red, yellow, and blue balloons together into an inflated crown and placed it on Callie's head.

"Thank you." She turned around, her full skirt swirling, and said, "Well, how do I look?"

"Like the Princess of Plymouth." Jason made a low bow. "Or should I say Miss Blueberry, the queen of the festival?"

"That was a long time ago." Callie handed the balloon man a donation for his ministry to children.

"Thanks. Jesus loves you," the man answered.

She'd forgotten how small-town people spoke His name so

easily. In Chicago, unless someone was swearing at traffic or a departing train, the word *Jesus* embarrassed people much more than a questionable website.

"You were a beautiful Miss Blueberry." Jason whirled her around. "You're even prettier now."

Warmth crept up her face. "Um, Jason—"

"Everybody knows it, so why shouldn't you?" He guided her to a coffee booth. "Want a doughnut, too?"

"No thanks." She knew he had to watch his pennies.

Along with a number of church members, they watched Pastor Sam and his family perform several songs in the market center. Each member played a different instrument, and most of them sang.

"A gifted bunch," Jason said, applauding and yelling with several youth group teens. "I'm glad we came to support them."

One of their high school teachers, now retired, stopped Callie and Jason to chat. It seemed all Plymouth had congregated at the farmer's market this Saturday, savoring their small-towness before thousands of Blueberry Festival visitors swarmed their streets.

"We're both going to get really busy. Me at the festival. You at Andrea's wedding." His hand tightened around hers. "Let's enjoy every minute together we can."

They eyed fresh loaves of white, rye, and cherry walnut bread baked by the nuns at nearby Ancilla College's Earthworks and wandered among a dozen booths that sold fruit and vegetables. Callie's mouth watered at the sight of bushels of corn. Nothing tasted like Indiana's fresh corn on the cob, dripping with melted butter.

They did split a sweet roll they bought at the Marshall County Cancer Association's booth and listened to a group of grade schoolers play scratchy violins. Lively seniors formed sets to square dance, including an elderly couple from Eastside. The wife, Millie, dressed in a poufy red skirt, gave her tall, thin farmer husband an I-love-you smile. His tanned, lined face shone as he returned it.

Callie's heart constricted. What would it be like to love like that? To stay sweethearts, even after forty, maybe fifty years?

Would she grow to care for Jason that much? Would he care for her? Andrea's reference to his quoting Bible verses during their fling still stung. Callie's sideways glances ran along his cheek, touching his thick, beautiful hair, measuring the length of dark lashes fringing those gorgeous eyes. *If I'm blind to his inner faults, Lord, please help me see.*

As if sensing her unease, Jason turned to her. "Are you upset?"

"Oh no. Just…sometimes I can't let myself be happy."

"I know what you need." He led her to a booth chock-full of flowers. "What kind do you like? What color makes you smile?"

"They're all beautiful—but I guess reds and oranges always give me a lift."

"Well, that narrows it down to only half of them." He grinned and grabbed an enormous bouquet of flaming gladioli. "How about these?"

"They're beautiful! Just one will be fine—"

"No, it won't." He paid the beaming owner—thank heaven, much less than he would have at a store or flower shop—and thrust the gladioli into her arms. Hugging the long, narrow stems of blossoms, she wondered how she could have let herself feel down.

"See? What did I tell you?" Jason took her hand. "I really like to see you smile."

They wandered a little longer then headed for his car.

She bumped her head climbing into the front seat. "Why didn't you remind me about the balloons!"

"I was afraid you'd take them off." He shut her door and then jumped in beside her.

She transferred the crown to his head. "Your turn."

Grinning like a five-year-old, he started the car. It began its usual mechanical convulsions.

Next time I'm going to suggest we take my car. As they left the market, she tried not to think how much his dilapidated lemon bothered her.

Nothing seemed to bother Jason today. "Let's go to the park. I feel like a Saturday morning swing."

"These flowers need water." She couldn't bear to think of their wilting.

"I have to drop some music by the church." Jason coaxed the car along.

"Maybe we can borrow an old jar from the kitchen, leave them there, and pick them up later."

They chugged up Michigan Street, waving at several people they knew. Jason waved at several they didn't.

"Come on, be friendly," Jason reproved her, his eyes twinkling. "This is Plymouth, not Chicago."

Callie couldn't help giggling. "Do you realize that we look like escapees from a cartoon?" Sputtering, smoking little car with crayon-bright flowers filling the front seat, driven by a balloon-crowned crazy.

"So what? It fits our Saturday morning theme. Besides, most of them waved back."

He even wore the balloons when they dropped the flowers by the church. However, Jason did shed the crown when they arrived at the park. "Moms here with their kids might think I'm weird."

Flocks of screaming small children ran, climbed, and chased each other all over the playground.

"They're darling. Though if we want time together, we'd better walk in the back of the park first," Callie said.

"Good idea. By that time, most of the crowd might go home for lunch."

The noise levels did not dip much after they crossed the covered bridge. Electrical workers, mounted on ladders and hydraulic lifts, tinkered with light poles. Carneys and crafts people were already setting up their booths. Little League teams, practicing for the festival tournaments, shrieked with soprano macho.

Jason slapped himself on the side of the head. "I was just here a couple of days ago. Of course, they're getting ready for the Blueberry Festival."

When a rumbling flatbed loaded with portable potties beeped and backed into an area nearby, she wanted to run away to the cool, quiet woods with him.

"The Greenway!" She'd never explored the trail because the city only recently created it. "Why didn't we think of it before?"

"With our luck this morning, bikes might run over us." He didn't look as enthusiastic as she'd expected. "Or the wheelchair bunch from the senior trailer park. I hear they're trying to set new speed records."

"Oh, come on." She tugged him around the first bend of the Greenway's wide blacktop path.

I was right. This is better than swinging. Although they encountered cyclists and other walkers, no eighty-year-old NASCAR wannabes in wheelchairs careened past. The river's summer song serenaded them as it wound gently through thick green foliage that shielded them from the blazing sun. She loved the fragrance of moist earth and the melodies chortled by smart birds who had taken refuge in the Greenway, too.

"This looks like a perfect place to run. Maybe when it's cooler and quieter, we can do a mile together." She grinned. "I might even beat you."

"I'd rather run on the high school track. Or out around Grandpa's." His eyes had darkened to slate color.

O-kay. What had changed his mood? She reviewed the morning. "Is something bothering you?"

"Of course not. I'm with you, aren't I?" He tickled the back of her neck—which he knew she couldn't bear—and she threw a handful of leaves at him.

When their mood quieted, they walked hand in hand, sharing their week, their faith, and plans to visit the Indiana Dunes State Park when the fall leaves showed off their loveliest colors. It should have been a perfect end to a perfect morning. Yet despite Jason's grins, his hand almost clenched Callie's, rather than clasped it.

Father, if he wanted to tell me, he would have. Please help Jason deal with this problem. If I can help him, keep me patient until the right moment.

His doldrums seemed to lift when they left the park, when he donned the balloon crown again. Why? Jason had been the one who suggested they swing that morning. As they picked up the flowers and drove home, Callie tried to put her finger on his odd behavior.

He'd seemed almost…watchful during their walk.

Watching for what?

Chapter 12

"Why are you here?" Jason had given up on subtleties.

Brandy shook her black mane free from its ponytail and touched her hand to her chest. "Me? I've been running this morning, same as you. We want to get healthy, don't we?"

"Right." Jason glanced ahead to his grandparents' front picture window, trying not to clench his fists. "You live close to the Greenway and near the high school track. So I thought maybe you just happened to run about the same time I did. But you don't live anywhere near here."

"Hey, it's a free country. I happen to like running along this road better than in town."

"I would appreciate it if you would stop stalking me." He gritted his teeth. "No. Let me rephrase that. Brandy, we have nothing in common anymore. *Stop stalking me.*"

"Is that the way for a nice Christian boy to talk?" Brandy slid him a reproachful look from under her lashes.

Fireballs exploded inside him. *God, help me end this once*

and for all. "We need to talk, Brandy. Once and only once. But not here." The run already had winded him. He gulped a deep breath. Another. "I suppose you won't meet with a pastor and me?"

"I wouldn't want to waste the preacher's precious time." She looked amused.

He thought quickly. "I teach this afternoon at Bethel College. Would you meet me around two-thirty at the Tradewinds Restaurant? It's near campus."

"I remember." She fluttered her hand at him, turned, and sauntered to the cul-de-sac where she'd parked her car.

He'd forgotten that Brandy had met him at Tradewinds during his early unspiritual days at Bethel. She no doubt remembered the motel, too—located a safe distance from the college.

So did he.

As Jason listened to the student play, he wished he could give him back his money. No way could he keep his mind on the kid's techniques today. He contented himself with offering an extra session with him the following week. The truth was, this student could use it. Jason loaded his briefcase, threw it into his car, and marched across campus.

Finally.

He'd rehearsed the speech a thousand times. He'd prayed through most of his students' lessons. Now, as he slipped through the campus exit to the nearby strip mall, he prayed as he'd never prayed before.

He walked to the restaurant, pushed its heavy glass door open, and scanned the dining area. No Brandy.

"Table for one?" A blue-jeaned teen server gave him an approving glance.

I wish. "No, another person will join me soon."

She looked disappointed, but led him to a booth in the homey mom-and-pop place. He drank several cups of delicious steaming decaf—he usually drank the real stuff—but he felt jittery enough.

And lonely.

Callie, if only you could have come with me.

Ha! As if that would solve anything.

Jason felt his face flame. Had he yelled out loud?

Hunching his shoulders, he cast a glance around the restaurant. Servers still brought food and chatted with customers. Students and a couple of professors read at several tables. He drew a sigh of relief and tried to read the newspaper he'd brought. But his mind wouldn't let him focus on foreign affairs or the funnies.

He wanted Callie to appear instead of Brandy, Callie crowned with those silly balloons, hugging fresh orangey-red flowers, her wonderful eyes full of life and laughter. He ached to feel her hand in his.

Jason looked at his phone for the fortieth time. If only he could fast-forward his life a few hours….

Finally Brandy appeared at the entrance, flashing her marquee smile. To his surprise, her dress looked almost conservative—certainly, by Brandy standards—until she turned to gesture to the server before she sat. He realized most of the back was missing.

And you believe we have a future? I can't think of a single place I'd want to take you. Instead, he wanted to hold up a sign: Take My Ex, Please.

"A diet cola," she ordered. "Hi, Jason." Folding her hands on the table, she leaned toward him. "So, how did your lessons go today?"

He guessed her conversation would mirror her dress: seemingly harmless, but deadly. "Okay. But I hope you don't mind if we skip the chitchat."

"Just being friendly." She turned a little sideways and leaned a hair closer. "We can be friends, can't we?"

The server arrived with her drink. He waited until the girl left. "No. I'm sorry, Brandy, but no, we can't."

"Why not? You liked me a lot in high school. Even when you started college here." She leaned on a long-nailed hand. "I think you still like me."

His palms felt as if he'd dipped them in warm water. He prayed beads of sweat wouldn't break out on his face like zits. "I care about you, Brandy. I'm sorry your life hasn't turned out the way you planned. I know what that's like." He gulped ice water. "But I'm a Christian now. Things can't be the same between us."

"*That's* being a Christian?" Her eyes widened in little-girl pain. "Turning your back on your friends when they're down?"

"If you want help, tell Jesus about your struggles. Ask His forgiveness for your mistakes." If only she would listen! "You know the Gospel—you heard it in youth group at least a dozen times."

"I bet *you* can't still say the Four Spiritual Laws. Don't you remember? We had to memorize them so we could go to Six Flags." She quoted them verbatim, laughter tainting her voice and eyes.

He wanted to close his. "You know the truth. I will pray for you. If you need a friend, I'll find a Christian woman who will help you—"

"Ooh, a woman like Callie."

Don't even say her name. He gripped the edge of the table.

"She might have been a Bible-thumper in high school, but I happen to know she wasn't such a sweet little angel in college. Or in Chicago." Brandy stretched across the table, leaning closer to him.

Now hot sweat dripped from his face. "Leave her out of this, please."

She was almost in his face. "I'll bet you two don't have anything like we did, right? Right?"

He tried not to shrink back. But he couldn't let her touch him—

"Well, if it isn't Jason Kenton. Good to see you." A small, bespectacled man, holding his coffee cup, had stopped at their table.

"Hello, Dr. Talmadge." Jason fell back into the booth as if released from a force field.

"I sure miss you in class."

"Yours were the best." He stole a glance at Brandy. She was staring at the gray-haired professor as if he were a reptile. "This is"—he almost said "my friend"—"this is Brandy Dubois. Brandy, this is Dr. Thomas Talmadge, a theology professor at Bethel."

"Hello, Brandy." Dr. Talmadge extended his hand. "Do you live here in town?"

She brushed it. "No. I'm from Plymouth, too."

"Has Jason shown you the campus? Bethel's a wonderful place."

"He's told me all about it," Brandy said hastily.

Dr. Talmadge continued as if he hadn't heard her. "We've been around now for more than sixty years and have developed many excellent programs, including adult studies...."

He launched into a detailed description of Bethel's history, departments, and accomplishments. Even Jason, who cherished his alma mater, felt his electrified nerves slowly dull. While the rest of Jason's surroundings faded, Brandy's wide-awake face didn't. Her mouth tightened to a thin line. Her eyes hardened till they looked like green marble. Still, Dr. Talmadge droned on and on, waving his hands to emphasize his points.

"Jason, I have to go." Brandy didn't wait until the professor paused for a breath. "I'll talk with you later."

"No," he answered. "I don't think so."

She stood and flounced out of the restaurant.

Dr. Talmadge cast a brief glance at her retreating bare back then sat in her place.

For a moment, Jason said nothing—only sucked in the free air. His professor sipped his coffee, as if they'd met to shoot the breeze.

Finally Jason said, "Thanks, Dr. Tom."

"You're welcome." The man's eyes behind the outdated glasses twinkled with a sudden shrewdness. "You were right to call me."

"I knew I couldn't handle this by myself." Jason shook his head and then gave a small chuckle. "How did you manage to sound so incredibly boring? You—one of the best teachers I ever had!"

"In a long academic career, you're bound to run into windbags." Dr. Tom grinned. "Not hard to imitate them."

They laughed, but the professor's smile faded. "That girl's real trouble."

"The worst. Unfortunately, I helped make her what she is." A wave of shame almost drowned him, but he fought through it. "I couldn't cut off all contact without one final appeal to her to turn to Christ. She needs Him so much."

"Yes, she certainly does." Dr. Tom leaned toward him. "But she doesn't need you. So limit your prayers for her to a maximum of once a day, five minutes or less. From then on, reject any thoughts of her and, of course, no contact whatsoever. Zero."

The professor's gaze held Jason in a kind but firm grip. "She will not be without prayers. When my wife and I pray for you—and you'll be on our daily prayer list—we will pray for Brandy. You no longer need carry that responsibility. God, who cares for her more than anyone, will send the right person to minister to her."

At his words, Jason felt as if a piano-sized weight had been lifted from his shoulders. "I hope she'll leave me alone. That I won't have to call the police."

"I hope you won't, either." Dr. Tom's mouth tightened. "But do it if you must."

Jason hesitated. "Would you pray for Callie and me, too? We've set boundaries in our relationship. We want to keep them."

"Sure." His professor searched his face. Jason felt as if those scholarly eyes were CAT-scanning his soul, but Dr. Tom smiled and said, "I'd like to meet Callie."

"I want to introduce her to you. She's an awesome woman." Night and day, the way he felt about Brandy and Callie.

"I'm sure she is." The professor looked at his watch. "Wish I could spend more time with you, but a faculty meeting calls."

They rose, and the older man rested a hand on his shoulder then clasped him in surprisingly strong arms. "You have my cell number, Jason. Don't hesitate to call me if you need help. You know the Lord will be with you every moment."

"Thanks again, Dr. Tom." Jason's grandpa hadn't hugged him in years. His dad lived in Texas. Nevertheless, he left the restaurant grateful that his Father had given him exactly what he needed.

Callie knew she shouldn't have drunk a diet cola on the way to Notre Dame. Why could other people buy a drink and arrive at interviews intact? Sitting in her SUV, she used the rearview mirror to help her scrub the blotch on her top with stain remover stick—she'd as soon leave home without it as she would her keys—but today the miracle didn't happen. She changed the length of her necklace. Better. She'd have to remember not to make big gestures, and she shouldn't drink anything else. Perhaps no one would notice. She would simply overwhelm the interviewer with her brilliance.

Callie winced at the distance she'd have to walk in heels.

At least she'd given herself sufficient time. Odd, coming as a potential staff member rather than a student. She lifted her eyes to the Hesburgh Library and the Golden Dome gleaming in the summer sunshine. Though she still felt the presence of the school loan elephant, the surrounding buildings reminded her of the strong academic base she'd gained here. Even from this distance, she reveled in the lush beds of geraniums and marigolds that spread their smiles throughout campus.

Wait. She cupped her hand over her eyes. The guy crossing the street, the one with that I-love-life stride, the golden wheat hair. *Jason?*

She almost yelled and then reconsidered. He probably was walking to a lesson. He'd told her the night before at youth group that he worked a tight schedule today. She checked the time on her phone. She should touch up her makeup and hair, and another scrubbing session might remove that stain. Besides, she needed to keep her mind on the subject at hand.

She'd almost reached the ROTC building, when she slapped her hand to her forehead. *Idiot.* How could she have forgotten her portfolio? She removed her pumps. If she ran, she'd make her appointment in time.

A moment later, however, she skidded to a dead stop, her heart pounding like drums at a Notre Dame football game. A tall figure wearing a dress with almost no back swayed down the sidewalk near the library, disappearing around a corner.

Brandy.

Callie had seen her only a few seconds, but there was no mistaking that long black braid and leggy walk.

Why is she here?

The hot sidewalk burned her feet. Unwelcome thoughts burned her mind.

Get moving, Callie. You have an interview to do.

Chapter 13

"Doesn't get any better than this." Jason stretched out on the blue- and lime-striped beach blanket, turned over on his back, and clasped Callie's hand.

Sitting beside him, she watched the sun play with strands of his hair, loved the golden lights in his smiling brown eyes. Despite his fair coloring, he didn't have to slather on SPF 50, as she did. *Not fair.*

Lying on the Culver beach only ten miles from Plymouth, he looked like the quintessential California surfer dude.

She raised her eyes to the indigo surface of Lake Maxinkuckee, whose waves met the achingly blue sky, separated only by a line of summer homes—a number of them movie-screen-grand—that circled the lake like a charm bracelet. Boats pulling skiers buzzed across the water. Little children in colorful bathing suits dug in the sand. On one side of the lake, a flock of small sailboats bobbed as cadets from nearby Culver Military Academy learned seaworthiness. A large academy yacht floated near, its rigging looking as complex as a calculus problem. *I'd flunk that class. I can't even untangle a necklace.*

A gorgeous day. Callie flopped beside Jason. Last summer she'd felt flat, lifeless, alone. Moving back to Plymouth hadn't even entered her mind. Lying on a beach with Jason Kenton? She chuckled. Even less likely.

Still, twinges of uneasiness, like ants crawling on her leg, kept her semi-awake. With college classes starting soon, Jason had grown much busier. They sneaked hours together like cookies from a jar. Would that change after he finished his master's? Maybe he could find a permanent teaching job nearby. He spent so much time running to Bethel, to IUSB, to Notre Dame—

Notre Dame.

The day of her interview floated to her mind's surface. She saw Jason again, walking to a lesson.

Why did she see Brandy there, too?

She sat up, breathing in the breeze, trying to regain the day's serenity. Okay, so both turned up on campus. *But why assume the worst?*

Maybe Brandy was involved in an intercollegiate project. Or she needed reference materials from the library. Or, more likely, she knew a guy there. Probably a dozen guys.

At any rate, she wasn't Brandy's keeper. Callie focused on her meeting with the department head. Despite the rocky start, the Notre Dame interview seemed to go well. The person she'd talked to sported a stain on *her* top, too.

"Want a cold drink?" Jason's voice dissolved her angst, as always.

With her hand in his, complications seemed so solvable. "Why don't I treat us to an iced coffee?"

"A cola would be fine with me."

She knew he didn't like her paying for anything, but he

needed to get over that. "I really, really want a frozen raspberry mochaccino."

"Maybe you really, really are a city girl." He let her pull him to his feet and tug him across the street to The Culver Coffee Company.

The remark stung a little. Maybe earning an excellent salary in Chicago had spoiled her. Still, she wished she didn't have to think about money with every small splurge. As they bought their drinks, she reassured herself that though she'd heard nothing from her interviewers, she'd receive a job offer soon. Surely someone would call.

They walked along the shady shoreline bordering the beautiful grounds and stately academy buildings, but the loveliness of the place didn't dispel another prickly question: *If Jason and I move on to a serious relationship, will I have to pinch every penny until it screams?*

"Are you upset?" Jason searched her face.

Rats. Already he read her moods way better than Ty. She hesitated then said, "A little concerned about finances. No callbacks from my interviews yet. I worry about paying off my huge school loans."

He laughed. "I learned a long time ago not to obsess about money. I don't think about it much anymore."

She'd figured that out already. Anybody who drove a car like his didn't lie awake nights planning his portfolio.

"The Lord has taken care of me so far." The postcard sky and water behind him, Jason smiled into her face. "Do you think He might be able to handle your financial challenges, too?"

She had to grin. "He does seem to have the rest of the universe well in hand, doesn't He?"

"I think," he said, "that we need to take your mind off such trivial matters." He stooped and picked up a flat rock from the stony shore. "I propose we hold the Great Rock-Skipping Challenge of the World."

She picked up another rock. "Mister, I don't think you know who you're dealing with. Andrea and I used to compete almost every day when we swam at Price's Pond." She flipped it sideways, watching it skitter several times across the water.

"I see I'm dealing with a pro. But that makes two of us." He frisbeed his rock, earning her applause and determination to beat him.

Laughing and teasing, they finally declared themselves co-grand champions and sat close together on a nearby bench. For a long time they held hands and watched summer happen.

"Girl, I can't figure you out." Aunt Sheila, her hips stuffed into her lawn chair, cocked an eyebrow at her daughter.

Who can? Callie, sitting next to Brandy on their deck, slapped at a mosquito that had escaped the purple-striped bug zapper.

Aunt Sheila obliterated one with a flyswatter. "You haven't hung around this house in weeks."

Brandy merely ground her cigarette into her mother's Florida souvenir ashtray.

Callie didn't get it, either. But she hoped her cousin, on hearing Callie was coming over that evening, had wanted to touch base. Maybe she'd hear how Brandy's class was going.

Her cousin lingered. Finally after listening to Aunt Sheila's latest diatribe against Uncle Alan—supposedly passed out in a bedroom—Brandy said, "Mom. Enough, already." She stood. "Callie, want to grab something to eat?"

"Sure." Twilight had drifted in—a little too dark for comfort. But two women together would be fine, especially since Brandy knew people. Still, Callie's city vision returned. Walking to the restaurant, she scanned both sides of the road.

"How's school going?" She decided to beat her cousin to the

draw. *She'll probably ask for more money. But I want her to succeed. If she needs cash for books or gas, I'll give it to her.*

"School is school." Brandy looked away. "I like South Bend. I like anything that takes me out of this crummy little town."

Aunt Sheila's gripes. Brandy's gripes. Callie sighed and kept walking.

Her cousin lit another cigarette. "Jason likes South Bend and Mishawaka, too. We both do."

Tiny prickles of fear, like burrs in a pasture, clung to Callie's thoughts. She blocked pain and irritation from her voice. "Maybe. Though he's glad to be back in Plymouth."

"You want to think that, don't you?" Brandy's husky laugh shivered down Callie's spine. "You want to think he's all shiny brand-new, a small-town boy who loves Jesus and loves you."

Inferno in her soul. Icy hand squeezing her heart. Callie called on her Mr. Stonewell experience. *PR voice. Use the PR voice.* "You may find it hard to believe, Brandy, but Jason does love Jesus. And I think he cares for me."

Brandy chuckled again. "Why don't you ask him about the last time we got together in the big city?"

Without another word, she strolled away into the darkness.

Checking e-mail at his grandparents' computer, Jason threw his arms up. "Yesss!"

"Good news?" The corners of his grandmother's tired mouth turned up.

"Awesome news." He danced her around the kitchen. "Dane Dodson wants me to open for him at the Blueberry Festival."

Even Grandpa, whom Jason thought was hypnotized by a *Matlock* episode on the den's big-screen TV, grinned from his monster leather recliner. "Maybe you're gonna go somewhere, after all, boy."

Jason grinned back and pulled out his cell.

"You calling that long, tall gal of yours?"

"Yeah. I've been waiting for an e-mail from Dane; she's been waiting for job offers."

"I recall she interviewed here in Plymouth and at Notre Dame."

You paid attention? Jason had brought Callie by only a time or two.

Grandpa shifted in his chair, sucking one of the lemon drops that helped him resist his pipe. "She's a nice girl." His eyes even twinkled a little under bushy eyebrows. "Maybe a keeper."

"I hope so." Whoa, two miracles. Dane had said yes, and Grandpa actually approved of him. Or at least, his choice in women.

"Let the boy call Callie." Grandma fussed at her husband. "It's time for your pills."

Leaving them to their bickering ritual, Jason ducked around the corner to his room and flopped onto the bed. *Thank You, thank You, thank You, Lord!* He could hardly wait to tell her.

Rats. Sent to voice mail. Why didn't she have her cell on? Maybe another interview. He called Andrea's home.

"She and Andrea left to run wedding errands," Mrs. Taylor said. "Probably to celebrate, too." The smile in her voice grew. "Callie just accepted a job offer."

"Thanks, Mrs. Taylor." He hung up.

Things are looking up, Lord. He'd run twice this week on the roads around his grandparents' house, with no sign of Brandy. He'd followed Dr. Tom's advice, and he felt as if he'd escaped a straitjacket. Dane had okayed his performance. Callie had found a job! *She won't go back to Chicago now.*

Where would they celebrate? He'd put his money on peach smoothies every time—and their favorite smoothie haunt, Java Trail. He'd pick up a few red roses and surprise her at the coffee shop. Of course, Andrea would turn up her nose at him, but he'd hug and high-five a little—then save the real celebration for tonight. Which would Callie like best, the Edgewater Grille or Corndance Cafe in Culver? The Emporium in South Bend? He decided to make reservations at the Edgewater. Callie had loved walking the paths along the lake and the military academy's campus—*"It looks like a little piece of Europe,"* she'd said. He'd have to scratch for gas money, but as long as his car didn't collapse until his next paycheck, he'd make it.

A phrase from the Psalm he'd read this morning bubbled up like an artesian well: "My cup overflows."

Yes it does, Lord. Mine is running over.

"Last thing on my list. Until I make another one." Andrea struck through "final flower conference" as they exited Felke's. "Hey, what's with you?" Her sharp eyes scanned Callie's face. "Wasn't Harper-Tarrington the job you really wanted?"

"Absolutely." Smiling about that was easy. "Great work, salary, benefits. Not the amount I made in Chicago—I didn't expect that—but here in Plymouth, I might be able to buy a house within a few years."

"Maybe next door to me." Andrea and Patrick were looking at properties on Nutmeg Road.

"I doubt it. Single income, remember?"

"That might change."

After Brandy's barb last night, Callie doubted it—at least, not soon. *Every time I start to believe in Jason, a new problem messes with my confidence.*

She turned her attention back to the road. For once, she had driven so Andrea could pore over her costs as they conferred, confirmed, and conquered.

"Didn't go over budget even once. Smoothie time!" Andrea stuck her smartphone into her bag and pumped her fist. "Take us to Java Trail, baby!"

"Yum and double yum!" Callie guided the SUV under the viaduct. Maybe a smoothie would help her shake off Brandy's sneering insinuations, at least to the point she could pull herself together, call Jason, and tell him about the job. He'd already called her three times today.

Callie parked in the lot next to the river. As she and Andrea yakked about their morning, Callie let her spirits rise. Free parking. Best friend. Now, a great job. Wonderful church, and a ministry where she could help kids find God and themselves. Last, but not least, an incredible guy. Plymouth was the place where God had led her. Why did she let her cousin bother her? As if Callie could depend on anything Brandy said...

Andrea entered Java Trail and came to a dead stop. Callie, who easily looked over her head, saw what had frozen her steps.

Arms thrown around him, but not Callie's arms. Full, poisonous lips pressed against his, devouring him. For a moment, Jason sat immobile, as if Brandy had paralyzed his body. Then he flung her off.

Other Java Trail patrons stared.

He cared nothing about spectators.

He saw only Callie, stunned by the same sting that nauseated him, her face bleached white, her eyes green like the sky before a tornado strikes.

She pivoted and escaped to the sidewalk, Andrea dashing after her.

He grabbed his roses from Brandy and sprinted out the door. "Callie!"

She ran as if he were the devil.

"Callie! Stop! Listen to me!"

Andrea, who had shorter legs, did stop. Guarding the street with a saber-sharp glare, she dared him to cross it to the parking lot. "Forget it, Jason."

Callie already had jumped into her car as if it were a getaway.

"But it's not like that—"

"I don't want to hear it. I'm sure Callie doesn't, either. If you've got a brain in your head, leave her alone until she cools down."

"She's not answering her cell—"

Andrea turned and marched away.

She was right. Standing like the wallflower at a middle school dance, he watched the car roar away. The potent perfume of roses made him sneeze, and a shower of limp petals hit the sidewalk. He realized he had crushed the roses to his chest. They scattered in the wind, leaving him with nothing but thorns.

Chapter 14

"You want to talk?" Callie addressed the geese pecking bugs from the grass. "So talk."

Only one goose of the dozen hissed at her as she rehearsed her lines. But five awkward gray adolescents trailed after the mother, so Callie forgave her protectiveness. Mama Goose reminded her of Andrea, hissing and pecking and flapping whenever Jason dared show his face—except at church the past Sunday, where both she and Andrea ignored him.

For several days, Jason called or texted Callie at least a dozen times daily. Each one stabbed her with new pain, anger, and longing. Sleepless, she finally responded, texting to say yes, she would be willing to meet. Briefly.

Fury boiled in her when for a full day, he made no reply. *Two can play at that game*, his silence seemed to say. Finally he asked when and where.

She suggested Ancilla, a Catholic college, convent, and retreat center a few miles outside of Plymouth. She arrived early and ran the rural roads around campus, pounding her frustrations under her feet. She also planned to pray awhile, as she did frequently as a teen. Once while bicycling, she'd discovered Ancilla's small mirror of a lake—its benches and wooden chairs strategically placed along quiet paths so a person could be still before God. No one blinked an eye if you sat staring for an hour. If you shed a few tears, no one minded that, either.

She especially enjoyed walking the prayer maze—except the goose population had increased, and now she had to do the Texas two-step to avoid yucky stuff. "Why don't you guys stay on the lake?" She imagined the nuns who ran the place shared her sentiments. "Although sometimes prayer *is* messy, isn't it?"

Why am I talking to geese, not to God? She'd fully intended to spend a deep, spiritual hour in prayer so He could tell her what to do. Now after walking the shoreline, hopping around the maze, and sitting on a nearby bench fiddling with her journal and pen that didn't work, she didn't feel any closer to answers. Or to God.

"Squonk! Squee-squo-squee-squonk!" The whole flock rose as if on cue. *"Hssss!"*

Jason, descending a slope to the lake, backed away as outraged parents flapped and accused him of attacking their young. If Callie hadn't been so upset, she would have rolled on the ground laughing at Jason's chagrined face.

"Come on." She motioned down a path. "Let's head to the woods."

"What was with them?" he asked when they'd found a quieter spot. "What'd I do?"

"No idea." Giggles she'd suppressed no longer vibrated against her ribs. *Maybe they don't like cheaters.* She pointed at a bench shaded by a large bush. "Over there?"

"Fine." He trudged to the bench and sat at one end without trying to meet her eyes.

Clearly, Jason wouldn't follow the repentant script she'd

written for him the past several days. Why was he acting like *she'd* done wrong? Callie sat at the opposite end of the bench.

They said nothing.

Finally, Jason broke the ice—with an arctic tone. "You said you wanted to talk. Well, talk."

She didn't like the way he'd grabbed her carefully rehearsed opening line. "Perhaps we should review the situation? You seem angry with me. If I'm not mistaken, you're the one who should apologize."

"Apologize?" He set his jaw. "Until you ignored my calls I was ready to, though I did nothing wrong—"

"Nothing wrong?" Callie crossed her arms. "Making out with my cousin in Java Trail—"

"I was not making out with her. I was waiting for you."

"Waiting for me?" All the hurt and frustration of the past few days—she couldn't seem to stop it—spewed out. "What's the matter, did you get bored? Most people just play with their phones."

He froze. Callie dared not say another word. It might be the one that would push him away forever.

He chipped his words out of the silence. "If you're at all interested in what really happened, I'll tell you. If not, I'll leave you and the geese to talk."

She didn't like the way he knew she'd been talking to geese. But she didn't want to lose the way he seemed to know her. "All right." She crossed her legs, her arms, and took a deep breath. "Tell me."

"I'd been trying to let you know that Dane has invited me to play at the Blueberry Festival."

"Yeah?" She hid delight behind careful nonchalance.

"Yeah." No warmth in his candy-sweet eyes. But did they soften the least little bit? Callie tried not to think of how she would have thrown her arms around him just a few days before.

"When I called Andrea's house, her mom told me you'd accepted a job offer. I wanted to surprise you—"

A big-screen picture of him and Brandy tightened her throat again. "Well, you did."

"I bought you roses." He ground the sentence in his teeth. "I figured you'd go to Java Trail. So I waited, hoping we could celebrate together and go out for a special dinner."

A small wheel of uncertainty began to turn in her stomach. "You didn't meet Brandy there?"

"If I were going to meet her, shower her with roses, and 'make out,' would I be stupid enough to do it in broad daylight? In one of your favorite places?"

She dropped her head, gripping it with one hand. Put that way, it sounded like the dumbest idea ever conceived.

"I don't know where Brandy hid. But she came out of nowhere and grabbed me just when you came into Java."

"How did she know you were there?" Callie cried. "How did she know you were meeting us?"

"Brandy's been stalking me for weeks." He groaned. "Mostly when I run—at least, I thought so."

He shook his head. "Not long ago, I read her the riot act, and I thought she had stopped. She must have been following me when I bought the roses and guessed they were for you. A little sneaking and conniving, and she accomplished her goal. Messing up what we have—or had." His voice broke, and he looked at his hands.

Anger and joy played tug-of-war with her heart. Not to mention humiliation. Callie wanted to cover her face. *But I need to know if you still care for Brandy. Or if you truly have given her up.*

She softened her voice to fit the peace of the rippling water and cloud-soft sky. "Jason. I have to know something."

"I've told you the truth." He raised his voice a notch. "What else do you want to know?"

"When did you last meet Brandy in South Bend?"

For a micro-instant, guilt crisscrossed his face. Raw, ugly guilt. Exactly the same expression Ty gave her when she'd asked him about his coworker.

"Callie—"

She rose and walked away.

Chapter 15

Cartons of purply blueberry ice cream, their untouched surfaces aching for a scoop. Ten-year-old Callie would have thought herself in heaven. But her adult counterpart behaved and followed orders. Working a shift at Eastside Church's booth, Callie plopped hundreds of scoops onto cones as thousands of hungry visitors streamed past. With rare picture-perfect weather this first day of the Blueberry Festival and more predicted for Labor Day weekend, attendance numbers probably would set records.

Good. I need to stay busy. I have to stay busy.

No more texts from Jason. No calls.

Andrea's wedding the day after tomorrow would keep her occupied. She wouldn't even have to think about Jason's performance Saturday night, because Andrea's dream day would arrive. White dress, fragrant flowers, loving vows, the first kiss for Andrea and Patrick as husband and wife… Callie's heart sank as if to the bottom of an ocean, but she forced it up to the surface to breathe. She wouldn't ruin Andrea's day.

Callie vented her feelings on the smeary stainless steel freezer, scrubbing it from top to bottom. She hoped her new public relations job at Harper-Tarrington, which started two days after the festival, would run her ragged. Scraping off gooey ice cream drips, Callie reviewed the facts about her new position, especially the salary. Enough that in the not-too-near future, she could scare the school loan elephant away for good, with plenty left over for raspberry mochaccinos whenever she wanted them.

Mochaccinos she would drink alone.

"Weren't you supposed to quit an hour ago?" Pastor Sam, hauling in another carton of ice cream, gave her a quizzical look.

"I don't mind doing a little extra."

"We've plenty of help now." He waved at her. "'Bye. Go have fun."

Forcing a smile, she left the booth, blending into the crowds touring the food stand aisles. Plenty of supper choices lined her way: philly cheesesteak, crispy fried walleye, polish sausage, pork chops, tacos, beans and cornbread, and enormous smoked turkey legs gnawed by happy little boys. Her stomach tilted like a carnival ride. She wanted nothing but to go home…though did she really want to face the Taylors' enormous, empty house?

She hurried past other ice cream booths, fudge, Dippin' Dots, and lemon shake-up stands—

A bright blue- and gold-scrolled sign on a stand near the end of a row greeted her eyes: Hort's Heavenly Elephant Ears.

Hort! She hadn't seen him in years. Callie jogged down the aisle, darting left and right to avoid collisions with people, strollers, and beeping golf carts. Finally she reached the small stand with its awning and white plastic tables. She remembered as a hot, dusty child taking refuge under its comforting shade, drinking cold water Hort handed out, eating little fried dough fragments he gave to hungry trailer court kids who had no money. Always teasing the children, Hort seemed like one big kid himself. *And you could tell him your troubles.*

"Hort! It's been ages since I've seen you—"

"Callie Sue! It's about time you showed up to say hi!" Standing in the window, he looked grayer, but his eyes never aged. "What a fine young lady you've turned out to be. You were such a special Miss Blueberry."

His smile made her feel better already. "Thanks, Hort. How are things going?"

"Been a wonderful year. Tell you about it as soon as I finish this batch." He dusted several golden elephant ears with sugar and cinnamon. "Want me to save one for you?"

"Thanks, but not right now."

She sat at a table watching him distribute elephant ears to the half-dozen salivating people who had lined up. *He's too busy to talk....*

Hort exited through the back of the stand, carrying two icy bottles of water.

"I'm sorry. You've plenty of customers—"

"I'll have you know, it's my break time." He gestured toward the stand and sat across from her. "My helpers can handle things awhile."

She gave him a grateful smile. "So tell me about your wonderful year."

"One of the best I've had in a long time." He paused, his smile fading. "You knew Kate passed away back in 2007?"

"No, I didn't." Callie wanted to hug him.

"Angie moved to the West Coast with her husband. So when my niece and her twin boys from California needed a place for a while, I offered to let 'em stay with me on the farm. Lauren's like a daughter to me. And those boys! Livened me up, all right." His grin couldn't stay hidden long. "She married a fine local boy last winter—Kyle Hammond—and settled down on his farm not far from me. So when the house seems too quiet, I know where to find all the noise I want."

"I'm so glad, Hort." No one deserved a loving family more than her old friend.

"How about you, Callie Sue?"

Looking down at her hands, she felt his kindly, keen gaze. "Not the worst year I've had."

"Not the best, though, right?"

Before she knew it, she'd poured out her story. Chicago. Ty. Quitting her job. Then she took a deep breath and told him about Jason.

"So Jason Kenton's turned his life around?"

"I—I thought so."

"He was a rascal, the whole time he was growing up." Hort shook his head. "I've known his grandpa for years. Kid was always makin' trouble. Tried to finagle free elephant ears out of me, though he had plenty of money. Thought he was God's gift to women."

Fresh rage flashed through her. "He says he's left all that behind, that he really wants to live for God. But—but lately, it doesn't seem that way." She didn't even want to mention Brandy. "I don't know if I'll ever trust him."

"Not a good feeling." Hort's knotty old hand covered hers. "But I can tell you one thing. I've seen Jason wandering around here today several times. He even came and talked to me. Whilst we were jawin', two little boys watched Tim in there making elephant ears." Hort motioned with his thumb toward the stand. "Just watched and watched. They didn't have any money. Jason bought them an ear apiece."

She bit her lip, trying not to cry. *And you worry about his attitude toward money?*

"Used to be, he'd walk by, his arm around a different girl every hour, it seemed. Today, no girls. Not even one."

No Brandy? Her heart leaped, but she said, "I'm not sure he'll ever speak to me again."

"We'll have to pray about that, won't we?" He patted her hand again and rose.

She checked the time on her phone. "I'm sorry I've monopolized your break."

"Glad we could talk for a little while." Turning, he threw a smile over his shoulder. "You never know what the Lord's going to do, Callie Sue."

She waved and rose from the table, then caught a tram and rode with other tired festival goers into the twilight. As the long wagon wound through congested streets, she gave thanks for Hort's listening ear.

Sometimes, Lord, I forget that You listen, too.

"Everything's ready." Andrea scrolled through her wedding files. "I've checked and rechecked. Nothing to do until the rehearsal tonight."

"Now you can take it easy." Callie knew better, but as Andrea's maid of honor, she should help her friend try to relax.

"If I sit home and think about what could go wrong, I'll worry all day." Andrea closed the files and flicked off the computer. "Let's walk around the festival together like we used to."

Even with knowing back routes to the park, they ran into traffic jams. Campers. Huge buses and Winnebagos. Lines of traffic, all converging on the high school parking lots, where orange-vested students and their parents parked hundreds of cars.

"Glad we don't have to do that." Callie tried not to remember the times she'd accidentally waved drivers into full lots.

The morning sun already beat down on crowds meandering among dozens of craft booths found in big tents, along the park's roads, and clustered near the carnival midway. Andrea pulled Callie from one end of the park to the other, determined to visit each and every one.

A galaxy of handmade, iridescent stained-glass ornaments glimmered in one booth. Beside it, a flea market entrepreneur sold T-shirts, Christmas wrapping paper, and velvet portraits of Elvis. One booth featured exotic-looking scarves, bags, and crinkled skirts. Another boasted hand-thrown pottery and another, exquisitely fashioned wooden boxes, shelves, and small tables. Callie and Andrea wandered among displays of Amish quilts, Christmas decorations, kids' pistols that shot marshmallows, custom license plates, potpourri, glow-in-the-dark masks, getups for goose statues, and thousands of other articles for sale at the Blueberry Festival.

Andrea pointed to a lamp whose glittery shade covered a fat-bellied chimpanzee holding a smashed can in one hand and a sign spelling out Party Hearty in the other. "I nominate this for my BFU Award."

"Definitely a possibility." Callie touched its fur. She and Andrea had conferred their private Blueberry Festival Ugly Awards since they were children. "I'm considering the fake shrunken head toilet paper covers back near the playground, but you never know when you're going to stumble onto a better candidate."

"Are you hungry?"

Callie smiled at Andrea's not-so-subtle question.

The fragrances emanating from food booths reminded Callie she'd skipped breakfast. "Yeah, I am." She asked the all-important question that topped every festivalgoer's agenda: "Where do you want to eat?"

"I have a special place in mind." Andrea gave her a little shove. "Come on, let's go this way."

Heated Little League, teen travel league, and women's softball tournament games already were in progress this morning. Fierce three-on-three basketball competitions raged on the blacktop courts.

For a few minutes they stopped to watch pig races. Pinkle Toes, a cute little pig with an extra-curly tail, caught Callie's eye. But Hammy Sammy, a black-and-white-spotted porker, beat out Sweatin' Like a Pig for the crown.

"Good thing I don't bet," Callie said.

They entered the covered bridge, jammed in with other pedestrians like stalks of celery. Callie tried not to remember a quiet, magic evening only weeks before when she'd crossed it with Jason, hand in hand. He probably was working somewhere in this mass of people...*please, God, don't let us run into him. Or Brandy. Especially if they're together.*

Ripping the image from her mind, she moved in front of Andrea, trying to keep her from getting trampled. Her friend shouldn't have to limp down the aisle. Plus, she'd trained hard all year to run the Stomp with Patrick.

Finally they emerged, passing the Ecuadorian Indian group wearing black ponchos and hats, playing their native pipe and guitar music. Several historical reenactment soldiers clad in wool Civil War uniforms, eating waffle cones, strolled by. Bikers clad in leather and bandannas made their annual appearance. Soon they would take off on their ride to support a cure for muscular dystrophy.

To Callie's surprise, Andrea's route veered away from the food booth aisles and toward the stage near Jefferson Elementary School.

Callie craned her neck longingly toward the delicious fragrances that teased her nose. "Why are we going this way?"

"All part of my special plan." Andrea steered her toward the stage.

"I don't want to watch arm wrestling!"

"That's later in the day."

No. It couldn't be. "You're not thinking…" She glared at Andrea.

"Oh yes, I am." Andrea beamed and stopped at an official-looking table. "We want to enter the Blueberry Pie–Eating Contest, please."

"*We?* I thought we decided in eighth grade that we were too old for this, Andrea."

"Hey, it was fun. Don't you want to do it just one more time with me?"

Blueberry Pete, a giant fuzzy blueberry mascot, cavorted around the stage.

Callie pointed at him. "You want to walk down the aisle looking like Pete in a wedding gown? You want purple faces in your wedding pictures?"

Andrea produced a small jar of petroleum jelly. "The stains will come off."

She'd planned this. Clear premeditation.

Of course the jelly would work for Andrea. But for her? With Callie's luck, she'd look as if she'd applied makeup with blue popsicles. "I really don't think this is a good idea."

"Just one more time? Pl–ea–ease?"

She'd wanted to make Andrea happy this weekend. Callie's mouth suddenly watered at the thought of juicy blueberry pie. "Well, all right. Maybe one of us will win."

They signed up and slathered on the greasy jelly.

She'd forgotten they had to sit on the stage—the ten adults who would compete before the children's contest. All were issued plastic ponchos to protect them from blueberry fallout.

Callie complained, "I feel like a toddler in a high chair."

"Quit griping," Andrea said. "Look at the pie. Concentrate on the pie."

It did look wonderful—a whole golden, crusty pie in front of her, with berries oozing from the curved cutout in the center.…

"Hey, Callie! Andrea!" Desiree, sitting in the front row of park benches arranged in front of the stage, waved.

"Yaaaay!" Austin roared beside her. "Go-o-o-o, Callie! Go-o-o-o, Andrea!" He stood up and led several other kids in their youth group in a cheer: "Two, four, six, eight, who'll have the biggest bellyache? Callie! Callie, *Callie*!"

The kid not only could sing—he could yell loud enough to be heard in South Bend.

Supporters of other contestants, not to be outdone, joined in a cheering competition. Blueberry Pete capered among the hopefuls. Andrea beamed through it all, as if the event were planned for her pleasure.

Girl, you owe me. Still, Callie couldn't help but grin and acknowledge her fans' support, clasping her hands above her head in an I'm-the-champion pose.

"Are we ready?" The master of ceremonies held a stopwatch. "You have one minute to eat as much of your pie as you can."

Callie poised her mouth above the pie's center. Spoons involved wasted movement.

"Ready. Set. Go!"

Her teeth chomped through the tender crust, raked tangy, juicy blueberries into her mouth. Munch, munch. More. More. *Mmmmmm.*

Maybe it was her starving stomach. Maybe the frustrations of the past six months drove her to gluttony. Or maybe she just wanted to be a winner again, not a loser.

Whatever motivated her, she soon stood at the front of the stage, sweet goo dripping from her face, with the master of ceremonies holding up her hand. Andrea and the youth group went crazy. Cameras and cell phones pointed at her, but she forgot about them as one pair of eyes—not berry blue, but toffee brown—met hers.

* * *

"Cal-lie! Cal-lie!"

He'd heard the youth group's cheer.

She hadn't believed he was innocent of wrongdoing. She didn't even wait for his answer to her question about meeting Brandy. Just walked away.

Yet today, hearing her name, he had to check it out. He couldn't help yelling, "Cal-lie!" along with the kids when she won.

The master of ceremonies announced, "Folks, I didn't know it, but our adult winner today is a former Miss Blueberry, Callie Creighton, who recently has moved back to Plymouth from Chicago. Welcome home, Callie!"

A roar of applause greeted his words.

She looks like she swam in pie rather than ate it. Jason wanted to fall on the ground and laugh himself silly. He wanted to cry. He hated gross youth group games, but right now he wanted to sprint to the stage, throw his arms around Callie's messy frame, and kiss her sweet, gooey purple face again and again.

Callie saw him. He didn't want to meet her waifish, unblinking gaze. But he couldn't tear himself away. *Lord, what do I do?* Should he walk away, too? Or should he eat humble pie again?

He decided to take the risk. Jason walked to the stage as Callie and a less disheveled Andrea descended the steps. The laughing youth group jumped around them like a mob of kangaroos.

"It's not my fault you forgot to use a spoon," Andrea said.

"You were awesome!" Austin cheered, but Jason noticed that he didn't try to hug Callie.

Jason edged in closer. "Uh, hello—"

"I think we'd better go home and shower." Andrea took a firm hold on Callie's arm. "My wedding rehearsal is tonight."

Callie said nothing. But she didn't let Andrea haul her away.

He held out the snowy handkerchief Grandma always made him carry.

"Thank you." Callie reached for it. Had she, for some reason, left her hostility back with the crumbs of blueberry pie? Because her eyes, though wary, answered his, rather than froze him out. Her hand met his, fragile fingers brushing his palm, oh so gently.

She tried to toss back goopy hair from her purple face and then rubbed it with the handkerchief. "I'll do my best to remove the stains and return it to you."

His heart turned over. He hoped that meant—unless she dropped the hanky into the mail—that she would talk to him again.

Chapter 16

Andrea was right, of course. Thanks to thick layers of petroleum jelly, 99.9 percent of the blueberry stain came off their faces. Callie dotted on extra foundation to cover a couple of small blue shadows. So far, however, soaking Jason's handkerchief in bleach hadn't removed the petroleum jelly and blueberry stains completely. But she'd think about that later.

Right now Andrea and Patrick's rehearsal commenced with pleasant clockwork precision. None of the I-thought-*you*-were-going-to-call-the-preacher kinds of disasters that plagued other rehearsals in which Callie had taken part. Everyone knew his or her role and performed it. Callie held and returned Andrea's shower-ribbon rehearsal bouquet on cue, straightening the bride's imaginary train at strategic moments. During the recessional with Patrick's older brother, she kept her steps small because he was three inches shorter than she.

At the delicious postrehearsal dinner hosted by Patrick's gracious parents, Andrea's glow of happiness out-lit the chandeliers in Christos' Banquet Center. Patrick, usually a model of intelligent self-possession, wore a goofy grin.

Watching them sideways from her seat at the head table, Callie wondered, *Is that what happens to guys when they truly fall in love?* She couldn't remember Jason ever wearing that slightly slack-jawed, happy "duh" expression.

Jason. *Will I ever stop thinking about him?* In this unmercifully romantic environment, she could no more wash him completely from her mind than she could wash the stains from his handkerchief. Would she return it to Jason? Not right away. She owned no picture of him. Later, lying on her pillow in the darkness, she could hold the handkerchief's softness to her cheek and wish things had gone differently.

Patrick's father told a joke that brought the house down. Callie framed a smile on her face, commanding her eyes to hold the appropriate sparkle. *Pay attention, you self-centered pie-snarfer! Don't let Andrea see a hint that you're hurting.*

She squeezed Andrea's hand and told the truth—that she was her best friend forever and she couldn't be happier for her. Callie turned to Andrea's cousin from New York, one of her bridesmaids, and made light, witty conversation, even enjoying the woman's company. After dinner Callie circulated among the couple's friends and relatives, determined to do her part to make Andrea proud and relaxed.

"What a perfect evening," Lana remarked after the last guest had departed. "Though it makes me paranoid about tomorrow."

"Oh, Mother. I think we have it under control." Andrea turned to Patrick and kissed him. "Don't let your brothers keep you up all night watching Adam Sandler movies, okay? I want you awake and smiling tomorrow."

He didn't say, "Yes, dear," but his dreamy assent made everyone grin.

Andrea's cell rang. "Oh wow, a cake-napper's stolen the cake."

Grinning, she clapped the phone to her ear as her mother and future mother-in-law chuckled.

"Hello…what? Well, get someone else. That's ridiculous; of course there's someone else…. Not on Blueberry weekend?"

Callie watched her friend shrug, and then demand, and then wilt. Her hand went to her head, dug into her temples. Oh no. Whatever was going on, Andrea just couldn't get one of her lie-in-a-dark-room migraines. Not on the eve of her wedding.

Andrea hung up, her smile faded into a sickly grimace. "The pianist for the reception received last-minute tickets for the Notre Dame game and cancelled on us."

"Wow, the game against Michigan?" Patrick and Rich both dropped their jaws.

Patrick said, "*Nobody* gets tickets to that game unless they're related to the pope."

"What*ever*." Her tone sent both back to the huddle of guys several yards away.

Callie and Lana each slipped an arm around Andrea in a silent, sympathetic hug.

"We'll work this out, honey," Lana said. "Don't let it worry you tonight."

"Maybe I'll stay up and watch Adam Sandler movies all night." Andrea clutched her temple again.

Should I call Jason? But Andrea blew up when she found he'd played at her shower. Besides, he's opening for Dane tomorrow night.

Aloud she said, "We'll call your organist and see if he can play. Or if he can suggest one of his friends—"

Now Callie's cell rang. Was it—could it be—Jason? Trembling, she checked the ID.

Brandy.

Callie's fingers curled. She wanted to ignore it. She wanted to flush the phone away in the ladies' room. Instead, she held it to her ear. "Hello."

"Callie?"

Her cousin sounded as if she was choking. Did Callie hear tears in her voice? Whatever her grief, she no doubt deserved it. Callie made herself answer, "Yes, Brandy?"

"I—I need your help. I'm in jail."

"I'm sorry, but I already told you I can't play tomorrow night."

Lounging on the tram he'd just parked for the night, Jason frowned at his phone.

"I wouldn't call you this late if the bride wasn't desperate," the Swan Lake event planner wheedled. "She's really in a bind now. I'm sure you understand how important this is to her and her family."

You have no idea how important my gig is to me. Give up opening for Dane and the Great Great Lakes Orchestra to play for Andrea Taylor's wedding? He almost laughed into the phone. Cicadas in the trees encircling the tram lot sang out the derision he felt. Andrea had done everything in her power to influence Callie against him.

Yet he couldn't blame her. Jason squirmed on the chilly plastic seat and heard himself say, "Look, if Ms. Taylor can't find anyone else, let me know. But don't tell her that."

He hung up and dropped his head into his hands.

Lord, what'll I do if they call me back?

"I didn't do anything wrong." Brandy, her cheeks stained with mascara, scanned the bare, featureless room as if looking for an escape route. She gripped the edge of the lone table. "I was visiting friends. Their friends—two guys I didn't know— started making meth in a bedroom."

Callie leaned across the table, trying to capture her cousin's glance. "Why didn't you leave?"

"Um—"

"Do you use meth, Brandy?"

"Is this an interrogation?" Her lips pulled back from her teeth. "I've already had it up to here with the cops. I don't need it from you."

"I'm sorry to upset you—"

"Do you think I'm stupid enough to use meth?"

You're stupid enough to end up here. Callie wanted to say it. She closed her eyes and saw Brandy again in Java Trail, her lips devouring Jason's, her body pressed against him.... *God, help me.*

"Stupid" wasn't what Brandy needed to hear. At least, not right now. Callie touched her cousin's hand and lowered her voice. "Did you take a drug test? That'll confirm you didn't use. Even if you didn't, the police found the meth lab at that house. From what your arresting officer told me, you could be charged with intent to manufacture, along with your friends."

"They got no proof I did that." Nevertheless, the flaming anger on Brandy's face paled to raw fear.

To Callie's own amazement, she walked around the table, sat, and slipped an arm around her cousin's tense shoulders.

Brandy turned and clung to her in a hug that nearly cracked her ribs. "Please get me out of here. Mom won't come. Please, Callie. I can't stand to be locked up."

"I can't do that." Callie rubbed her back, tried to relax the arms that bound her like wire. "The officer also told me they usually charge you and assign bail within forty-eight hours, but that the holiday may slow things down. Since you're on probation, they can hold you here without bail for several days."

"But I haven't done anything wrong." Brandy pulled back so fast Callie almost fell off the chair. "Can't you find a lawyer who will get me out of here?"

She hesitated, feelings of guilt sweeping over her. "I want to help you, Brandy, but—bottom line, I can't afford bail costs or legal fees. The court will assign you a defense lawyer at your hearing if you need one."

Brandy's hands clenched at her side. "I told you, I can't take being locked up. Can't you do *anything*?"

Callie tried not to clench hers. "I can let your folks know where you are."

Brandy rolled her eyes. "Thanks *so* much."

The sarcasm seared Callie like acid. For a moment, she thought of walking away from Brandy forever. *But You never turned Your back on me, Lord.*

She said quietly, "I'll always be here for you."

Groaning, Brandy sank into her chair.

Callie covered the weeping woman with her arms, her heart. "You're my cousin. I'll visit, and I'll never stop praying for you."

The next morning Callie decided to close the jail scene with Brandy as she would a bad YouTube video, along with any mental pictures of Jason. *Focus on Andrea,* she told herself. *Deal with problems after the wedding.*

Sharing the joy that permeated the church nursery turned dressing room, Callie didn't find it too difficult.

"My wedding day." Andrea turned so her mother could fasten the tiny buttons on the back of her billowing white dress. "I wondered if it would ever come."

Callie lifted Andrea's filmy, elegant veil with its tiara of pearls from the shelf it shared with toddler storybooks. She placed it carefully on Andrea's head. "I think you made the right decision about leaving your hair down."

Lana pinned the tiara while Callie shifted the big oval mirror they'd brought from home so Andrea could see. She fluffed the bride's train and handed her the exquisite bouquet of white lilies, roses, and ivy.

Oohing and aahing with the four bridesmaids, Callie stood back and admired.

"Oh, Andrea." Lana cupped her daughter's face in her hands and kissed her. "You are so beautiful."

Andrea, her cheeks a soft blush pink, wore her mother's pearls. In her dress and veil, she resembled a grown-up fairy princess.

Thank heaven the event planner found a pianist. Callie was brushing her teeth upstairs when she'd called just after breakfast with the good news. No other problems had emerged— so far.

Today Andrea's eyes, which often sparked with fireworks, looked almost serene, like blue ocean pools. They sought Callie out, and she hugged her best friend.

No words needed. I'm not sure they could say what I'm feeling anyway.

Lana broke up a giggly group hug. "Goodness, look at the time. We'll need to line up in fifteen minutes."

A flurry of smoothing hair, dresses, grabbing white lily bouquets. Catching a glance of herself in the mirror, Callie once more felt a surge of gratitude for Andrea's good taste. Callie's sleek sea-blue maid of honor dress with its tapered, ripply hemline followed classic lines. No bunchy ruffles or lumpy satin flowers in all the wrong places. The other bridesmaids' dresses were a few shades lighter.

Quickly they formed a line. Rich, handsome in a black tux, hugged and kissed his daughter. They walked to their position at the end, Callie fussing with Andrea's train and veil.

Andrea leaned close to her ear. "I have a special surprise for you."

"What?" Callie had endured enough surprises the past weeks.

"You'll know it when you see it. I think you'll like it." Andrea held out her pinky finger.

O-kay. Still, Callie linked it with hers. With a little wave, she took her place.

Watching the other bridesmaids gracefully process down the aisle, she prayed. *Lord, I know You'll help me face all the sadness tomorrow. Today, help me put it aside and rejoice in my friend's happiness.*

Chapter 17

I don't think Callie sees me yet. Jason, sitting near the back of the church, tried to remain anonymous behind a tall guest and his wife, who wore an elaborate hat.

It reminded him of hiding behind plants at Andrea's shower. If nothing else, dating Callie had taught him basic espionage.

Maybe he shouldn't have come to the wedding. But Andrea and Patrick had invited him, and he wanted to honor them.

As he listened to the vows, songs, and prayers, he prayed, too. *Lord, thank You for this opportunity to heal past hurts. Please bless their marriage in every way.*

When he'd made his decision to play at Andrea's reception, he'd called the event planner and then held his breath as he phoned Andrea herself.

"Aren't you opening for Dane tonight?" She'd sounded as if he'd lost his mind.

"This is more important," he'd answered. "If you'll accept it, I'd like to make this my gift to you and Patrick."

Andrea babbled several incoherent sentences to express her thanks. He expected the later call from her with a song lineup for the reception. He didn't expect an invitation to the wedding.

"I've talked to Patrick, and we'd both like you to come."

At her words, an invisible chain broke. He felt he could breathe again. "Thanks. I—I may take you up on that." Blown away by Andrea's openness, he nevertheless wondered if he should attend. "Please don't tell Callie until after the ceremony. I don't want our complications to mess with your wedding."

"I won't." Through his cell, he could hear Andrea inhale a deep breath. Another pause. Then, "I'm sorry I blamed you for everything."

"I'm sorry you had reason to blame me. Happy wedding."

"Thanks." An awkward, but not uncomfortable silence. "Well, good-bye."

"Good-bye."

Now he hid in his seat near the back. Still, he couldn't resist peering around the couple in front of him. If he slid so he could peer past the edge of the woman's hat, he could see Callie better, especially when she and the best man joined Andrea and Patrick in facing the congregation. Hopefully the hat wouldn't draw her attention to his peekaboo game. Jason felt the curious glances of older couples sitting on either side of him. He pretended sitting sideways was normal and caught glimpses of Callie that made him want to run to the front, stand beside her, and say, "Can we do this, too?"

Finally, Pastor Sam pronounced them husband and wife. Jason rose with the other guests and clapped as Andrea and Patrick, wearing exuberant smiles, led the recession toward the sanctuary's exit. Escorted by the best man, lovely Callie, also wearing a genuine grin, stopped dead in the middle of the aisle, causing her escort to stumble over his feet like a grade school kid. He barely kept from falling on his face.

Jason winced. She'd seen him. Too late to hide under the pew.

Her eyes bulged, and her mouth stretched into a perfect O. For once, she did resemble the "Fish Face" nickname he'd given her.

A camera flashed. Andrea's photographer had caught her and the best man at exactly that moment. Another unique portrait for Callie's photo album, unlike anyone else's on earth.

Jason packed every ounce of love he felt for her into his eyes, his smile. Would Callie, alias Fish Face, alias Miss Blueberry, open her heart to him once more?

She was hallucinating. These past weeks finally had sent her over the edge.

Jason. Looking so good, she wanted to dip him backward for a Hollywood kiss.

Hollywood kiss? The Java Trail video played again, helping her recover and march out of the sanctuary, eyes straight ahead, to stand in the receiving line with her annoyed escort.

Her lips offered Patrick's brother a hundred apologies, but her mind repeated a different monologue in an endless loop: *Jason, why did you come? How dare you upset Andrea on her wedding day!*

She smiled, helloing the people she didn't know, hugging and kissing most of the ones she did, praying Jason did not possess the nerve to wish Andrea and her groom a wonderful life together. Or to hold Callie's hand and look into her eyes—

He walked up to Andrea. Took her hand. *Noooo*—

Andrea greeted Jason without animosity. So did Patrick. In fact, they seemed downright cordial.

I'm dreaming this. Too many sausage and pepper sandwiches at the festival. Too many rich hors d'oeuvres at the rehearsal dinner last night. And way too much Brandy.

Now he was shaking hands, moving down the line. He

clasped Callie's cold hands in his warm ones, those melting brown-sugar eyes thawing her way too fast—

He leaned in, his whisper tickling her ear. "Can we talk for a minute when you're done?"

Noooo. "Yes." He continued quickly, the bridesmaids' gazes following him out the church's front door.

She'd just qualified for Pushover of the Year. But if Andrea's welcoming smile for him was real…Jason's words might prove important, words Callie needed to hear.

She continued greeting guests, trying to show genuine enthusiasm at their how-pretty-you-look comments, trying to remain a good sport when they teased her about her need for coordination lessons.

She breathed a sigh of relief when the last of the crowd paraded past. She turned, wanting to grab Andrea and shake her to sensibility: *"What is with you? That was Jason who took your hand. You smiled at him!"*

But Andrea and Patrick were preparing to dash out the door. Callie, along with the other attendants, formed an aisle at the head of the gauntlet of wedding guests.

Patrick's brother—who really was a nice guy—counted, "One. Two. Three. Go!"

The bride gathered her train. The groom threw a protective arm around her, and they ran madly through a blizzard of birdseed and good wishes to a white limousine.

Her heart racing, too, Callie secretly monitored groups of people standing near the doors. Many guests exclaimed about the lovely wedding. Others made their way to their cars.

But Jason, entering the church again, walked straight toward her.

He'd watched Callie kiss all those people. He'd had to restrain himself from kissing her just now. If only he could hold her and never let her go.

Jason shook himself as he approached her. Enough, already. He had to say all the right things—in about two minutes.

He halted at a discreet distance. "We have a lot of things to work out. I–I'd really like to talk to you."

She stared at him. "Fine. Maybe then I'll understand why you came to Andrea's wedding. And why Patrick and his groomsmen didn't toss you out."

"First, Andrea and Patrick invited me."

"O–kay." Callie shrugged. "Maybe, with the prenuptial stress, they went crazy, too."

"Seriously." He cleared his throat and gestured toward armchairs off to the side of the foyer, where they sat. He lowered his voice. "I know it's hard to believe. When the event planner at Swan Lake tried to talk me into playing for her reception, I told her no, of course. But the longer I thought about it—and prayed about it—the more sense it made. If Andrea allowed it, I could show her I was sorry for messing up her life."

"But Dane—"

"I canceled. He seemed to understand the situation. I'm hoping to contact him later about other gigs."

She said nothing for a moment. Then, "You did that for Andrea?" Seemingly dumbstruck, she searched his face.

Yes, I did it for your friend. And for you. "I knew God forgave me for hurting her, but I needed to do this. I called her, apologized, and offered to play." He glanced at his watch. He'd better hurry this up. "I think she understood what I was trying to do, because she not only accepted my offer, she and Patrick invited me to the wedding. I came to honor them." He paused. "And because I couldn't stay away from you."

"I—I've missed you, too." Her cheeks flushed pink.

A thrill of joy spiraled up his spine. "I've missed you so much. We need to talk—"

"We do, but not today. I'm due early at Andrea's reception."

"So am I. I can hardly wait to watch you all evening while I play without a jungle of plants blocking my view."

She giggled. He chuckled. So good to laugh together again.

He wanted to keep things light, but they needed to take care of important business. "How about talking over elephant ears tomorrow?"

"I have to work at the church booth in the afternoon."

"I have to drive a tram."

Delight sparkled in those emerald eyes. "Your grandpa asked you to drive?"

"He did." Saying it made him feel like a million dollars.

Just as quickly, her eyes turned blank as glass. "Jason, to-morrow I—I have to visit Brandy."

"Visit her?" He'd rather be shot. "Why?"

"She's in jail. The police think she was manufacturing meth."

No surprise there. Still, Brandy's sad mess of a life touched him. If he'd stuck with that lifestyle, he'd probably be serving time, too.

Instead, this evening he'd celebrate Andrea and Patrick's love—and hope for the resurrection of his and Callie's budding romance. Glancing at his watch, he said, "Why don't we work out our elephant-ear date on the way to the reception and leave the heavy stuff for tomorrow? I'll give you a ride."

"Sorry, I'd better drive myself." She looked genuinely disappointed. "I'm sticking around till the end to help Lana and Rich clean up."

"Maybe I can lend a hand, too."

"You don't have to."

He'd do just about anything to bring them closer together, but he'd better not push too hard. "I'll ask the Taylors for their take on the situation."

They exited the front doors. He'd parked down the street and slipped in late to sit in back and blend in with the crowd.

Her SUV sat in the opposite direction, only a few spaces from the front sidewalk. He stood close to Callie, yet without touching her. The faint fragrance of her citrusy perfume made him dizzy. He'd been dreaming of a moment like this for days.

I don't want to leave her. Not even for the thirty-minute drive to Swan Lake.

"See you in a little while," Callie said.

He started to turn. Her fingers touched his arm, setting it on fire.

Watching her walk away, he remained until she opened her door. He made himself jog toward his.

She not only stole his breath away, she'd stolen his heart.

He didn't want her to give it back.

Callie had practiced the toast daily for weeks. With Jason watching her from the piano, though, she wasn't sure she could remember her name.

Oh, he'd remained discreet. A professional performer, with that flashing smile, he seemed to make guests feel as if he'd played a song just for this couple or that grandma. Yet she knew him well enough—when did that happen?—to sense a current between them she could feel through a wall.

She didn't want to lose that warm, electric flow. Though she did manage to pull her thoughts in, mentally rehearsing the speech's beginning and end, reminding herself to stand up straight. She scanned the lovely candlelit room, noting that many guests still were eating the delicious beef burgundy and chicken scaloppine. She'd wait another fifteen minutes or so before the toast.

"Having a good time?" Andrea's voice made her jump.

"I am." She stuck out her pinkie finger.

Andrea linked hers with Callie's. "Did Jason explain? He wouldn't let me tell you—"

"He told me the gist after you and Patrick left. You really

did give me a surprise. An incredible one." Her voice broke a little. "Thank you."

"For what?" Andrea's smile faded. "I made things impossible for you."

"Don't say that. Especially today. Your day." Callie touched Andrea's lips. "Nothing will make me happier than to see you forget all that and have the time of your life. Deal?" She tugged gently on her friend's pinkie finger.

"Deal." Andrea reciprocated.

A tableful of Andrea's old Manchester College buddies began banging spoons on their goblets, so Patrick claimed his bride for a kiss as Jason launched into, appropriately, Faith Hill's hit, "This Kiss."

She hadn't heard him play country before, but he did so wonderfully, as he did Bach, Beethoven, the Beatles, and Beyoncé. His eyes gleamed at her across the room as he played, and she wondered if she would last the evening. Maybe she should borrow plants again. She drained her water glass and decided she'd waited long enough to begin the toasts.

Callie poured sparkling grape juice from the bottle near her plate into Andrea's glass and then into her own. Patrick's brother, catching her signal, also poured juice into Patrick's and his goblets. She stood, picked up the wireless microphone from the edge of the table, and announced the toasts, inviting the guests to join in.

After gurgles from the bottles subsided, Callie faced her best friend, glass half-full so she wouldn't spill it, but with an overflowing heart.

"Andrea, I want to say that you've been there for me all my life. From the time we first laid eyes on each other in kindergarten, you shared your Cabbage Patch doll with me, your Barbie car, your nail polish, and your cute new dress—until I hit a growing streak, and our system didn't work anymore—maybe about seventh grade?"

The guests giggled. Andrea grinned, but a corner of her mouth quivered.

"You also shared your parents with me." Callie raised her glass to Lana and Rich, sitting with relatives nearby. "Thank you for taking me under your wing. All of you have made me feel like family. If you hadn't opened my eyes to a wonderful world, I might never have seen it that way."

Lana touched a tissue to her eye and threw a kiss. Rich beamed, and Callie thanked the Lord once more for such amazing friends.

"Most of all, Andrea, you shared your faith with me. If you hadn't introduced me to Jesus, I might never have come to know Him. Because of that, we are sisters—even closer than biological sisters—both now and forever."

A tear trickled down Andrea's cheek. Callie fought hers back. "Now I will gladly share you with Patrick, a wonderful Christian guy, and celebrate your joy together." She raised her glass.

Andrea was crying now—thank goodness she'd used waterproof mascara—much as she had when they'd won the county soccer championship as eleven-year-olds. As guests toasted the couple, she rose and hugged Callie, who finally let loose her own tears. *Thank You, Lord, for my forever friend.*

Gentle piano chords crept into the room as they sat, and Jason's voice said, "I've put words of the Bible to music in a love song for this wonderful occasion. May I offer it now?"

A song? He'd written a song for this? When? How?

Cuddled close to her groom, Andrea nodded. Wonder flowed over Callie with the music.

Rise up, my love, my fair one,
*   And come away.*
For lo, the winter is past,
*   The rain is over and gone.*

Flowers appear on the earth;
The time of singing has come.

Come away, come away.
You have stolen my heart, my bride,
You have stolen my heart.

Don't assume too much, Callie. He's singing this for An-
drea and Patrick, remember? Jason's eyes rested on them.
Did he mean to detour the words from his heart to hers? She
tried not to revel in the melody, tried to push away the words
before they became a part of her.

She was failing....

Women dabbed their eyes. Couples reached for each other's hands. Patrick, usually so reserved, looked into his new
wife's teary face, his own glowing with joy.

With the fading of the last chords, silence lingered in the
room, begging for more.

Oh, Jason. If he'd sung one more note, she would have
run to him.

A crash of applause didn't seem to touch him. He was looking at her now. At her.

Finally the best man stood and turned to the groom. "This
is one hard act to follow. Still, I'll try my best not to make
you cry, Patrick," he promised, giving everyone a laugh. His
reminiscences, involving running away together and cherry
bombs at Bible school, brought the house down.

Callie had hoped the laughter would break the spell Jason
had cast over her. But one note from his piano, one glance
from those eyes, and she knew that wasn't true.

You need to think, Callie, not just feel. Think and pray be-
fore you talk to Jason tomorrow.

She tried not to let the magic take her over, even when Jason
grabbed a break to bring her a piece of wedding cake, saying

little, but offering a smile that made her crazy. Even when Andrea aimed her bouquet straight at her, and she caught it, burying her nose in the delicate fragrance of lilies and roses. Even when she could not stop humming "Come Away, My Love," as she gathered table decorations and candles afterward.

Her efforts fell short because Jason, stacking chairs and carrying boxfuls of gifts to the Taylors' van, filled her thoughts, her senses, even as he gathered trash.

Afterward he walked her to her car.

"See you tomorrow at Hort's?"

She nodded and watched him go.

Then she collapsed into her driver's seat.

It's going to be a long, long night.

Chapter 18

"You'll eat an elephant ear today, won't you?" Hort pretended to glare at Callie through his stand's windows. He grabbed a handful of dough and brandished it like a snowball.

Callie giggled. "Of course I will. I even skipped the church booth's ice cream so I might buy one. I'm just waiting for someone."

"Oh." He winked. "I think I saw Mr. Someone earlier today. He was playing the keyboard for a bunch of kids doing a puppet ministry. I saw him again around lunch time, pushing a lady's wheelchair when she got stuck in a rut. That's the only lady I've seen him with."

The sun didn't come out, but ripples of warmth swept her cheeks anyway. "You don't have to spy on him for me, Hort."

"I'm glad." Hort handed her a bottle of water.

"Thanks." On a hot, muggy day, nothing tasted better, especially when served with Hort's reassuring smile.

"Why don't you sit and rest? Do you good—especially if you and your fella are going to talk."

"How did you know that?"

"Not hard to guess. Ladies need to talk things out if they have issues on their minds. Us fellas need to learn to talk, too. We all need to listen, right?"

People crowded around four of the six tables housed under his awning. He gestured at one in the far corner. "Better grab that one while you can. Don't worry, I'll mind my own business. No eavesdropping." He grinned. "When you're ready for elephant ears, I'll fix you nice, hot crisp ones."

"With cherry topping." Almost drooling, Callie sat. "At least, that's the way I like mine."

Even the vision of a cherry-topped elephant ear vanished, though, as Jason approached and stopped at Hort's stand.

He wore jeans and a T-shirt. No romantic songs, no bouquets, no wedding ambiance surrounded them. But the magic still did.

Until she realized a sixtyish man and woman stood at his side. *Who are they?* She rose, wondering if he'd just run into them.

"Hi, Callie." Jason gestured to the couple. "I'd like you to meet Dr. Thomas Talmadge and his wife, Dr. Linda Talmadge, professors at Bethel College. He teaches theology, and she leads the nursing program. Dr. Tom and Dr. Linda, this is Callie Creighton."

"I'm glad to meet you," Callie said. They looked almost like twins with their matching smiles, twinkling eyes behind their glasses, and wavy silver hair.

"I'm glad to meet you, too." Dr. Linda's smile widened. "Jason asked us to pray for you two."

Callie felt her cheeks flushing again. "Um, thank you. Have you checked out the festival?"

"Yes, we've never come before," Dr. Tom answered. "Had

a lot of fun exploring. Actually, though, I came to share something with you about Jason. Do you mind if we sit?"

"Of course not." Of all the possible scenarios she'd imagined for today, this hadn't entered her mind.

"Time to hit the craft tents. I'll meet you in front of Jefferson School in a half hour or so." Dr. Linda kissed her husband on the cheek.

Jason sat across from Callie, his eyes pleading for her to listen. "I know Brandy told you about meeting me near Bethel. I brought Dr. Tom to tell you what really happened."

O-kay. She shifted her gaze to the professor, who smiled at her confusion.

"I know this must seem a little strange. I'm the one who told Jason I should talk to you. You see, Jason took several classes with me at Bethel. As a brand-new Christian, he asked me to mentor him, and we've grown quite close. He told me this former girlfriend, Brandy, was causing him difficulty and asked Linda and me to pray."

Callie leaned forward, almost crumpling the water bottle.

"Jason told me he'd arranged this final meeting there because he didn't want to be seen with her in Plymouth."

"Partly because I knew people would assume we were still dating, but mostly because I thought you would misunderstand." Jason shook his head. "I should have told you about it."

"I'm not sure I could have handled it." Callie found it hard to look him in the face, but she did. "In fact, I'm sure I wouldn't have."

The professor continued his story. "Knowing Brandy's tactics, Jason asked me to be present, incognito, at the restaurant where they met. I witnessed their entire meeting. It was a difficult one."

"I'm sure." Part of her marveled at Jason's wisdom. Part of her imagined only too well what Dr. Tom meant.

"Jason told Brandy they couldn't be friends and urged her to accept Christ and turn her life around. She had dressed inappropriately and used every wile in an effort to tempt him. I interrupted and essentially bored her to death until she left."

Any other time, Callie would have chuckled at the picture he painted. Now she said slowly, "He needed your help to say no to her."

"Yes, I did." A slow, red stain spread across Jason's face. But he did not lower his eyes.

"We all need help at one time or another, Callie," Dr. Tom said gently. "That's why God gives us to each other. The point is Jason has changed. If he hadn't, he never would have asked me to come to the meeting. He cared enough about the Lord—and about you—to ask for reinforcements so that he might win this battle."

The professor stood. "I won't intrude on your evening any further." He grinned. "Besides, if I don't hurry Linda away from those craft tents, she'll buy them out, and I'll have to carry it all to the car."

Jason stood and hugged Dr. Tom. "Thanks for everything. I really appreciate it."

Callie offered her hand. "Thanks for coming. For your prayers. And for being Jason's friend."

The professor smiled and left. Hort stuck his head out the window. "You ready for those elephant ears?"

"Sounds good." Callie had tensed her shoulders until they ached. Now she dropped back into the chair.

Jason brought the steaming treats to the table, covered with cherries.

"You like cherries on yours, too?" A little afraid to meet his eyes, Callie distributed napkins and plastic forks.

They ate without speaking awhile, the nonstop hum of conversation and echoes of a nostalgia band's "I Want to Hold Your Hand" in the background.

I should say something reassuring. But what? The snack diminished her drained feeling. At least she should be able to think now.

Jason looked less stressed, too.

She ventured, "I didn't expect you to show up with two professors."

"I know." He nodded. "Though when Dr. Tom proposed the idea, it made sense. I wanted a concrete way to show you that by God's grace, I've changed." He grimaced. "I know I'm definitely a work in progress—"

"Actually, I've achieved perfection myself." She buffed her fingernails against her shirt.

"Oh really?" He grinned, but his eyes glinted. "Is that why at Ancilla you walked away from me with no explanation?"

She bowed her head. "That didn't solve much, did it?"

"No, it didn't." He chewed the last piece of his elephant ear and placed his hands on the table. "You were going to tell me something that day. What was it?"

She fidgeted. "I—I was going to say you looked guilty when I asked you about meeting Brandy. My ex-boyfriend, Ty, wore exactly the same expression when he told me about his affair with a coworker. That I would just have to live with it while he 'explored his options.'" Callie gritted her teeth. "I hated that look on his face. I couldn't bear it on yours."

"So you judged me entirely by an expression." Jason crossed his arms.

"Not entirely." Callie looked him in the eye. "Do you remember the date you saw Brandy?"

He raised his eyebrows, but consulted his phone. "Let's see, that's the day Chad called me at the last minute to cancel his lesson. Here it is. August 10th."

She consulted her phone. "That same day, I interviewed at

Notre Dame. I saw you walking on campus from a distance, but couldn't talk because I was running late." Her stomach knotted. "A few minutes later, I saw Brandy headed in the same direction."

Jason's shoulders fell. Slowly he shook his head. "I didn't know she followed me. She must have lost me on campus." He lifted his chin. "If you're asking if my Tradewinds setup was all a fake and I met her again at Notre Dame, the answer is no. No, I did not."

Callie touched his cheek. "I believe you."

His eyes studied hers as if scrutinizing a new music score. Then he touched her face. "I believe that you believe me."

Callie lost track of how long they sat, soaking in each other's trust.

Hort's voice from the window brought them back to planet earth. "Are you ready for elephant ear number two?"

Jason raised his hand. "Bring 'em on. You want more cherries?"

"I barely finished one." She laughed. "I hope you're hungry."

Beaming, Hort brought fresh ones. "Enjoy and celebrate. Okay?"

"Okay." Jason said it at the same time she did. Grinning, they bit into the yummy ears. Callie ate a little, but extending her hand, she touched Jason's lips with a large fragment. The look on his face took her breath away. Slowly he ate, not moving his eyes from hers.

Yesterday, could she have dreamed of such a moment? She never wanted it to end. Yet deep inside, she knew what she had to do.

"Jason, I need to tell you something."

"All right." He took her hand.

She stared at her paper plate. "I'm sorry that I've insinuated our problems are all about you and your past. I've hidden from you who I am, or who I was."

He shook his head. "Callie, you don't have to tell me—"

"I think I do." She forced herself to lift her gaze. "After preaching at you and Brandy throughout high school about your sins, I proceeded to try most of them in college. In Chicago, I bought into the no-commitment-necessary lie. Ty and I would have moved in together, except for the fact we couldn't stand each other's apartments and habits. That should have raised a few red flags." She shook her head. "It didn't."

"I've achieved perfection, myself," he deadpanned, brushing his shirt with his nails.

She chuckled, even as her eyes teared. "I didn't get it until one Christmas Eve, when I finally grew sick of the office parties, the emptiness, the sham of it all. I begged Ty to go to church with me. He refused, but I went anyway. A little church in my neighborhood welcomed me, a stranger, that night as if I were family. The pastor spoke about God sending baby Jesus to give us a second chance. I didn't say much to anyone. I certainly didn't 'go forward' or anything like that. But a tiny spiritual shift took place inside me—a tremor that grew into an earthquake. A year later, Ty and I broke up."

She was crying now, and unlike Andrea the night before, hadn't used waterproof mascara. Jason dabbed at her tears with his napkin—probably making the smear worse—but she didn't care, because compassion shone in his face, which made her cry all the more. He kept dabbing.

She finally stopped—only to look around and notice the tables around them had emptied. She felt her cheeks flame and stood. "I'm scaring away Hort's customers."

"Hort isn't worried." The kind elderly man brought a pile of napkins. "Feeling better, Callie Sue?"

"Callie Sue?" Jason's expression morphed to the junior high version of his smile.

She shot him a junior high don't-you-dare-call-me-that look, then a grateful gaze to Hort. "Thank you, I'm feeling much better."

She scrubbed at her face. "After a little repair, I think I'll feel like walking around the festival. Nothing quite so energizing as your elephant ears. And your prayers." She stopped and squeezed his hand.

"Glad to share both." He winked and returned to his stand.

Jason rose and offered her his hand. "May I?"

"Absolutely." Her heart sang as she clasped it. So what if her makeup had gone AWOL? Jason knew she wasn't Miss Airbrushed, but he still wanted to walk with her.

They'd only meandered a short distance when a band began to play a heavy metal number that wrinkled Jason's forehead. "Not my style."

Callie shuddered. It sounded like a song Brandy would love. *Brandy.*

Smiling with her customary malice, Brandy forced her way to the front of Callie's thoughts. She saw Brandy again at the jail, clinging to her like a barnacle.

"Earth to Callie." Jason peered into her eyes. "Is there a problem?"

She held her hand to her forehead and closed her eyes. "I promised Brandy I'd visit her today."

The glow on his face vanished as if she'd thrown a switch. After a moment, he said, "I promised Dr. Tom I'd avoid her."

Since they were being honest, she said, "I don't want you around Brandy, either."

"I'll drive you to the jail and pray while you visit her." He pulled her close. "Then we'll come back to the festival, okay?"

"Okay." Callie leaned on his chest, feeling those strong arms encircle her. Hand in hand, they caught a tram to the parking lot and, after his car had coughed itself awake, drove to the Marshall County Jail.

* * *

As Jason and Callie walked to the front entrance of the new building, she looked through him with those amazing eyes, then halted. "What's bothering you?"

She'd zeroed in on his panic. How could he have thought he would fool her?

"It's tough for me to come here." He shook his head. "When I was seventeen, I spent two nights in the old county jail when Mom and Dad finally refused to rescue me. I'd been driving drunk. I deserved it. The experience probably kept me from landing there permanently. Or landing in the morgue."

She said softly, "You can sit in your car."

"I'm not the same guy." He gave her a gentle push forward. "I don't have to react like him."

"All right." She seemed to understand he needed to do this for himself, as well as for her.

They checked in with the front desk officer, who told Callie that after prisoners were booked, visitors saw them by video only. The officer offered to take her to the booths. She turned and squeezed Jason's hand. "I'll pray for you."

What a woman. He'd come to support her, and she'd pray for *him*? "Back atcha."

He moved to the far end of the lobby, which probably appeared spacious to other visitors. Every time Jason blinked, however, the walls closed in on him. He pulled out his phone and touched his Bible app to Psalm 119:45: "I will walk about in freedom, for I have sought out your precepts."

Christ had set him free. He wasn't about to let this place scare him out of helping Callie.

He read another psalm. He prayed for Callie. He played Angry Birds and then prayed again.

The walls began to back off.

* * *

"You have to get me out of here." Tears streamed down Brandy's pale face.

Callie's eyes widened. When was the last time she'd seen her cousin without makeup? Brandy peered at the camera like a bedraggled sparrow.

Pity lodged in Callie's throat. "I'm so sorry. I know it's hard—"

"No, you don't." Brandy glowered. "You have no idea what it's like. They dragged me out of bed at six this morning! For what? Because that's breakfast time—though I never eat breakfast." She tugged on the sleeve of her orange prison jumpsuit. "I hate this thing. I *hate* it." She let loose a shower of tears and profanity.

So orange isn't your favorite color, and you had to get up before noon. Callie, realizing her thoughts weren't exactly Christlike, corralled them in a prayer. *God, I don't know how to help Brandy. What do I say?*

"They tell you when to eat, when to go to bed. You're supposed to just do it, like a robot!" Her nostrils flared. "I can't get on the Internet or even watch TV."

She recited a long list of grievances she'd probably rehearsed every waking moment. Callie cringed. *Shades of Aunt Sheila.*

When Brandy finally paused for breath, Callie wedged in a small suggestion: "The officer said you might receive a few more privileges if you cooperate."

Brandy almost spat. Given her cousin's present attitude, Callie figured she'd have to kiss the shopping channels goodbye forever.

"When are you going to get me a lawyer?" Brandy almost snarled at her.

What part of "I can't pay your legal fees" don't you understand? Callie drained the anger from her voice before she answered. "I'm not going to find you a lawyer, remember? That's up to the court."

At first Callie thought Brandy would yell to the guard that she wanted to return to her cell. After an initial glare, she appeared to try to calm herself.

Probably because I'm her only visitor. Upon hearing of Brandy's arrest, Aunt Sheila had exploded, swearing she'd leave that girl in jail till she rotted. Uncle Alan had grabbed a six-pack and disappeared.

As the flame in her cousin's eyes faded to gray ashes, Callie searched for a subject that wouldn't turn controversial. Not chitchat about Andrea's wedding. Brandy had hated her for years. Not Callie's new job. Brandy envied every opportunity Callie ever earned. Spiritual subjects? At this point, counterproductive. Callie certainly wouldn't mention Jason's name. She aimed a prayer heavenward for him, for Brandy, for herself.

School. Maybe she could help Brandy with that. "Do you want me to contact your prof at IUSB?"

Brandy's eyes shifted past her. "Nah. Somebody will tell him why I'm not coming to class."

Brandy's lying look. Callie had seen it a thousand times. So Brandy probably dropped out. How long ago?

Still, today the fate of a few hundred dollars seemed like nothing.

"Callie?" Brandy's voice lost part of its edge.

"Yeah?" Callie leaned forward, but caution whispered in her ear.

"Have you gone to the festival yet?" She sounded nonchalant, but a tiny wistful note hid among her words.

"Mostly I've worked at the church booth."

"This is the first year in my whole life I haven't gone." Brandy's shoulders drooped. "Last year I didn't have money to buy one of those awesome bags, the ones with the silver beads and sequins. The woman who makes them always sets up near the Bill Nixon Baseball Field—"

"Yeah, those are gorgeous." For a moment, Callie fell into the rare girl-talk mode she and her cousin occasionally shared as teens.

"Would you get me one?" Brandy's eyes moistened.

"Sure. I'll keep it for you until your release." *Which might be a long time.* Tears welled up in Callie's eyes, too.

"Yeah, they won't let me have it here." Brandy's eyes flashed. "No bag, no jewelry, no clothes, *nothing.*" Her hand on the table clenched.

"They'll have to let me out soon, won't they? They don't have a shred of evidence against me."

Callie sighed. "I'm afraid it isn't that simple. With your record and the fact you violated your probation by associating with known meth addicts—"

"I'm telling you, I didn't do anything!" Her cousin slammed her fist on the table. "But you want to believe I'm bad, don't you, Callie? You always have. You're glad I'm stuck in here so you can have Jason." Panting, Brandy's breath almost whistled between her teeth.

Callie gripped the edge of the table. The thought had crossed her mind more than once. At this moment, she'd love to leave Brandy here forever. *Lord, help me. Help her.*

Curbing her angst, Callie took a slow, deep breath. "I know you don't believe me, but I care about you, Brandy. I'll keep praying for you."

Her cousin turned away, her shoulders set like a statue's. "Save your breath. I've heard all that Sunday school stuff. Bottom line—God hates me and always has."

"Time." The brawny woman guard in the background stepped toward Brandy.

Sadness swelled in Callie like a dying tide. Rising from the chair, she couldn't think of anything to say.

"Callie?" That tiny wistful note in Brandy's voice again.

Callie turned back to see Brandy standing near the lockup, the guard's hand grasping her arm. Her cousin hesitated. "You'll come back to see me, won't you?"

A miniscule light, like a candle in a dark harbor, glowed in Callie, then grew stronger. "Of course I will, Brandy. I won't give up on you. And neither will God."

Chapter 19

The minute he saw Callie, Jason wanted to storm the jail and force Brandy to apologize.

Probably not Your plan, Lord, right? Still, as they walked back to the car, Callie's tears tore through him. He wanted to restore the magic they'd shared at Hort's. Opening her door, he said, "Need another elephant ear?"

A minute smile sneaked onto her lips. "I don't think so."

"Maybe watch a good old down-and-dirty Little League game? We can yell at the umpires."

"That might feel good." The smile grew. "I guess part of trusting that God will take care of Brandy—and us—is acting as if we believe it. I don't feel festive, but I think we should return to the festival."

"Your wish is my command." He maneuvered the car through traffic, and soon they sat on bleachers watching fierce nine- and ten-year-olds compete for the festival championship.

Jason and Callie yelled their lungs out. But he doubted the

umpire heard them. Eloise Campbell, a lady from Eastside with a mouth as big as her heart, bellowed when her grandsons batted and fielded.

A ballgame, a sausage sandwich, a promenade through the park with Callie, and he was flying high, like the brilliantly colored hot air balloons sailing above.

"Someday I'm going to ride in one of those." He watched a green and yellow balloon float across the sky as if it wanted to meet the pale moon rising along the horizon.

"I'll fly with you." The look she gave him sent his heart soaring.

They crossed to the midway and rode the Paratrooper, the Octopus, and a merry-go-round of swings that whirled them in circles until even Jason thought a break might be wise. They tossed a miniature basketball and then threw rings and darts. He insisted on trying to win her a goldfish because she'd never owned one.

"Do you want to carry it all over the park?" Her practical side showed up.

"Hey, there are guys walking around the craft tents carrying chests of drawers." Jason gave her an injured look. "I'm only carrying a blanket for watching the fireworks. I think I can handle a goldfish."

Actually, he won two. They couldn't determine their gender, but she named them the Blues Brothers.

"Goldfish aren't blue." At times her logic escaped him.

"The guys in the movie weren't, either."

She made sense in a weird sort of way. He grinned. "Name 'em whatever you want."

"I will. Blue One, here"—she held up one plastic bag—"has a spot on his tail. Blue Two doesn't."

"Perfect." He meant it. Perfect name for the fish. Perfect girl. Perfect evening.

* * *

The mellow sound of voices and acoustic guitars wafted through the air, drawing Jason like the fragrance of a fresh-baked pizza. They walked toward the amphitheater, where gospel artists gave their concerts. Where Dane and the Great Great Lakes Orchestra had played last night. Where Jason was to have opened for him.

"You made Andrea's dreams come true. Mine, too, because I didn't want to spend that evening without you." Callie hugged his waist. "I wish I could say incredible words instead of 'thank you.'"

"You just said them." He hugged her back. "Want to listen awhile?"

"I'd like that."

They and the Blues Brothers sat on a bench. An older man sang "Amazing Grace" as his nimble fingers played a bluesy accompaniment on his guitar.

'Twas grace that taught my heart to fear.
*   And grace, my fears relieved.*
How precious did that grace appear
*   The hour I first believed.*

The Lord has promised good to me.
*   His word my hope secures.*
He will my shield and portion be,
*   As long as life endures.*

Wrinkles crisscrossed the man's leathery cheeks. Jason read the singer's story in them and in his gravelly voice: a hard, sad life for years. But the glow from within made his lined face seem like precious parchment. *Thank You, Lord, for rescuing both of us.*

Jason sang along. Callie's soprano lilted softly through the twilight. Others around them sang, too, and even from Randolph Street behind them, passing festivalgoers joined in:

When we've been here ten thousand years
  Bright shining as the sun.
We've no less days to sing God's praise
  Than when we've first begun.

Amazing grace, how sweet the sound,
  That saved a wretch like me,
I once was lost but now am found,
  Was blind, but now I see.

She nestled her head on his shoulder. He wanted to stay here with God and Callie and the Blues Brothers and the saved-by-grace singer forever.

The concert ended. Callie heard Jason whisper a prayer. Her mind echoed another. No one had ever prayed with her like this, holding her so tenderly.

Finally she said, "We should thank the singer."

They did, and he received their gratitude with unselfconscious delight. "Thanks for singing with me. I think the Lord had a real good time with us tonight."

As Callie and Jason walked across the meadow-like expanse in front of the amphitheater, scores of lightning bugs gathered in the growing twilight, putting on their own light show.

Thousands of people walked before them, behind them, beside them, converging on the park center to watch fireworks: families pushing strollers, their little ones decked in glow-in-the-dark jewelry; packs of boys, dashing about like puppies; clumps of laughing teens laden with stuffed animals; older people toting blankets and camp chairs; and young couples like themselves, small oases of just-we-two quiet. Jason squeezed her hand. Did he, too, wonder if they would walk the festival together in coming years, pushing strollers, corralling children, calling teens on their cells, seeking a large spot for their extended family to gather for the fireworks?

Don't get carried away, she reminded herself. *A few days ago, you didn't even want to speak to Jason!*

Threading their way through the crush, they passed Hort, who gave them a big smile and a wink to match. "Hurry! Before long, you won't even find standing room."

She kept up with Jason's stride as they turned near the tennis courts and found an empty spot where they spread their blanket. He set the Blues Brothers beside Callie. His arm slipped around her. She snuggled against his chest. Was that his heart thudding faster and faster, or just her own?

"Evening star." Jason pointed to the sparkling crystal chip in the cool, deep blue sky.

"Wisely keeping its distance from all this craziness." Callie wondered if Andrea and Patrick already had returned from South Bend for the Stomp tomorrow. Were they cuddled up, too, somewhere in the vast crowd?

"Ah, but it's missing all the fun." Jason offered his bag of kettle-cooked caramel corn.

"Tell it that when the fireworks start booming." Callie crunched the popcorn's sweet saltiness, absorbing the midway's costume-jewelry lights, the expectant multitude's murmurs. She inhaled the sweet September coolness of the night, the cedar-y fragrance of Jason's aftershave.

"Balloon Glow before fireworks." His arm tightened around her.

They turned to watch a dozen hot air balloons clustered together like enormous bubbles in one corner of the field. First one lit up, then another, then another, alternating patterns, blushing with color and radiance. She and Jason joined in the *"oohs"* and *"aahs"* all around them.

"Beautiful," she murmured.

His warm fingers tilted her face up to meet his gaze. "Not nearly as beautiful as you."

She caught her breath.

They'd talked, worshipped, struggled, fought, reconciled. Already they'd shared difficult times.

Were they ready to share the joys of togetherness without crossing boundaries they should keep?

Yes. She sensed it.

Yes. His eyes told her he did, too.

Jason slowly drew her to him and placed warm, gentle lips on hers.

She thought she would melt through the blanket into the ground. When he finally drew back, the balloon glow reflected in his face—or did the balloons borrow their light from Jason's smile?

The first *boom!* of the fireworks cracked the sky open like a piñata, spilling a shower of red, blue, green, and purple sparkling confetti. Huge golden dahlias and silvery daisies bloomed against black velvet. Enchanted hearts, flags, fountains, and rockets filled the night. Though she and Jason both brought earplugs *("A musician has to take good care of his ears," he'd said),* the *booms* didn't disrupt her happiness. Instead, they sounded like the joyful beats of a big bass drum in a parade that celebrated everything good in her life.

Boom! I found my way back to God.

Boom! I made the right decision in moving back to Plymouth.

Boom! I found a love I never anticipated in a million years.

Boom! Boom! Boom!

* * *

Too bad he had to return to work tomorrow. *How will I survive an entire day without seeing Callie?*

Carrying camp chairs a step behind her as they followed the parade route Labor Day morning, he knew he'd make it through the usual lessons and Starbucks shift. He just didn't want to.

Dressed in jean shorts and a bright lavender shirt, she looked as awesome as she had at Andrea's wedding.

Maybe a little time-and-space distance was a healthy thing.

"There they are!" Callie waved at Rich and Lana Taylor.

"Here, on the west side of Michigan Street, the sun will shine in our eyes before long." Lana apologized. "Still, how else will we see Andrea and Patrick when they run by?"

Jason set up the chairs while Callie took juice drinks from the Taylors' cooler. A ton of Andrea's relatives from the wedding had remained in town. They all greeted Callie and him kindly. The Blueberry Stomp runners hadn't passed yet, so the parade wouldn't arrive for a while. Several of Andrea's little cousins played Go Fish on a blanket near the curb. A few watched a video on a parent's phone. While Callie chatted with the women, Rich introduced a giant bag of blueberry doughnuts and announced his opinion that Notre Dame would remain undefeated this season. Two Michigan alums in the group hotly denied it. Jason talked and laughed as if he'd known these people all his life.

"Here come the runners!" Townspeople and visitors several blocks up the street stood, and like a football crowd doing the wave, applauded as hundreds of 15K, 5K, and 1-mile runners ranging in age from preschoolers to septuagenarians filled the street.

"Do you see Andrea and Patrick?" Lana bounced up and down for a better view.

"Not yet!" Callie yelled.

The Taylor horde jumped, shrieked, and waved in vain. No one spotted the couple.

"Maybe they decided to skip it?" Jason dropped into his chair beside Callie's.

She snorted. "Andrea's been training for this for a year. No way is she going to skip it."

"We'll spot them much more easily when they loop back this way toward the finish line," Rich consoled his wife.

A chorus of sirens blared, and the kids along the curb covered their ears. "Fire trucks are coming!"

They waved as every fire truck and police car in Marshall County joined in a slow-moving, light-flashing spectacle that signaled the beginning of the parade.

Jason relived his high school career when bands marched past. The rumble of the percussion, the power of the brass—he'd played trumpet—made him want to join the ranks. The teacher in him, however, wanted to correct their marching and show them how to play those high notes!

Soon his favorite nonmusical entry approached: the Culver Military Academy's Black Horse Troop. They seemed to walk naturally in sync with the music of the high school band, strutting their stuff behind them. As a kid, Jason had watched the horses on TV. They participated in presidential inaugural parades, proud heads held high, as they were now, flowing manes and tails stirred by the breeze.

The kids on the blanket loved the fezzed Shriners riding those crazy miniature motorcycles. Cute little local majorettes and gymnasts showed off their talents for the judges nearby.

The Miss Blueberry float approached. Callie tugged on his arm and whispered, "Do you know where we're sitting?"

"Um, Michigan Street. In Plymouth, Indiana. In the Western Hemisphere." What else was he supposed to say?

She giggled. "Lana and Rich just happened to choose The Place."

The Place? He had a lot to learn about the way her mind worked. "Why do you call it that?"

"Don't you remember? Ten years ago, this is where I fell off the Miss Blueberry float in front of the judges, God, and everybody."

He didn't know whether to grin or console or—

She laughed harder. "I'm sorry." She wiped her eyes with her hand. "It's just so much fun to laugh about it. I didn't think I ever would."

Gesturing toward the float, he said, "None of those girls rate anywhere close to *my* Miss Blueberry."

"You're not only cuter than you were ten years ago, you've gotten smarter." She gave him the smile that made him glad he was sitting down.

"First 15K runner!" The cry went up and down the street as a guy about Jason's age zoomed past to cheers and applause.

Clowns, Scouts, classic convertibles, and handshaking politicians followed floats and bands on the east side of the road while clumps of other runners thundered past on the west. Clapping and *"woo-hoos!"* greeted the first woman runner to return. More runners of every size and shape. Meanwhile, as cheerleaders, church groups, and a bagpipe band went by, Lana spent more and more time on her feet. Callie joined her, hand cupped over her eyes.

"I see them!" Andrea's mother leaped high in the air. "I see them!"

Yelling like a cheer block, the group rose and waved. Andrea, wearing a white T-shirt with Bride and some sort of lacy bodice printed on the front, waved back with an ear-to-ear smile. No frozen glance leveled at Jason like a poison-tipped icicle. He didn't have to hide from her anymore.

Patrick, wearing a black tux T-shirt, appeared to be sweating more than his new wife.

"Andrea looks better than Patrick," Callie whispered. "I don't think he trained as hard as she did."

Jason felt sorry for the guy. He'd have to move at Andrea speed the rest of his life. Judging from Patrick's grin, though, he didn't mind.

Out of the blue, Callie asked, "Want to run the 15K with me next year?"

"Whoa, that's a long race." He liked running a few miles, but more than nine? That would take a major commitment on his part—

The flinch in her face, faint, yet pained, grabbed him.

"Yes," he answered firmly. "Yes, I'd love to." He gestured with his head toward the couple's back, now several blocks away. "But I'm a long way from doing what they're doing."

"You and me both."

He knew they weren't just talking about running. His past, her past, Brandy's problems…how would they handle all those challenges?

"Andrea and Patrick could probably give us a few running tips. And"—she threw him a sideways look—"Dr. and Dr. Talmadge might have advice for us."

He nodded and took her hand again. "Maybe we could start training together next week?"

"Sure." She bent close to him and whispered, her warm lips touching his ear—"Your Bible or mine?"

Epilogue

One year later

Callie, sitting on the grass, stretched her right leg in preparation for the Blueberry Stomp. She basked in Jason's gaze as they warmed up.

His smile almost made her forget she'd soon be running nine miles. "Well, Mrs. Kenton, what do you think of married life so far?"

"If the next seventy years are anything like the first three days, I think I can handle this."

"At least your pianist didn't run off to the Notre Dame game."

"No, I'm kind of glad he stuck around." She touched Jason's cheek then shifted and began to stretch her left leg.

Jason had wowed her and their wedding guests with a mini-concert, playing "Come Away, My Love" and their other favorite songs, including more original compositions.

She'd spilled her drink before they toasted each other, of course—it wouldn't have been her wedding without some sort of mishap. But the sparkling grape juice hadn't splashed her dress, the graceful mermaid style she'd spotted in Treat's window when she first came to town. Otherwise, their day had gone without a hitch. Instead of cake, she and Jason had asked Hort to make his heavenly elephant ears, and the guests gave him a standing ovation! Even Andrea had liked the silvery-gray bridesmaid dresses with pink accents. (Desiree had been much easier to please.) Austin's strong young voice led worship during the ceremony.

Jason, so handsome in his black tux and silver vest, vowed lifelong love to her, his words serious and deliberate, those toffee eyes melting her with their warmth and sweetness.

If only Brandy had come to their wedding, Callie couldn't have imagined a more wonderful day. She bit her lip. Thank the Lord her cousin had been charged with a lesser crime than her friends. Callie's difficult visits with Brandy while she served her six-month sentence had gradually morphed into bearable and then even to friendly. With the Talmadges' blessing, she and Jason had tried to cultivate a good relationship with her. However, she'd disappeared the past two or three weeks. When Callie hopefully scanned the congregation during their ceremony, she'd spotted Aunt Sheila—who wouldn't, in that purple- and silver-sequined dress?—and Uncle Alan, who stayed sober, his wedding gift to her.

But no cousin shared her day.

"You're thinking of Brandy again, aren't you?" Jason pulled Callie to her feet.

She grimaced. "If you're reading my mind now, what will you do when we're old and gray?"

He leaned forward and rubbed his nose against hers. "I'll still be discovering new, awesome things about you."

"Like the fact I have to sleep with socks on?" Her feet always registered twenty degrees below her regular body temperature.

Austin's loud interruption saved him from answering. "Hey, Callie, Jason. Ready to have your picture taken?"

"Almost." She pulled a compact from her gym bag and smoothed her hair and lacy white T-shirt.

"Women." Austin rolled his eyes then bumped knuckles with Jason. "You were great Saturday night. Dane was right. You *are* the greatest thing to come out of Plymouth since him and blueberries."

"Stop it, Austin, or he won't be fit to live with." She had to smile, though. Bless Dane for offering another Blueberry Festival opportunity.

"She has to live with me for a long, long time." Jason winked.

Desiree, who had been talking to a couple of teen runners, took Callie's bag.

"Thanks for coming." Callie opened the box she'd brought and gently pulled out her short bridal veil. "I really need your help with this."

Desiree, who'd possessed a knack with hair since forever, practically nailed it to her head with hairpins. Callie said, "If I don't die from running nine miles, I might die from this."

"You'll do great." Jason pulled a top hat from the box. Striking a Cary Grant pose, he said with a British accent, "Come, my love; we'll astound the world."

"Or at least, Andrea. She didn't think we'd pull this off." Callie couldn't help her wicked grin.

They walked to the Centennial Park entrance and posed for Austin's camera. Prior to their wedding, she and Jason had posed under the arch for the wedding picture she'd always dreamed of. Somehow, her album also needed this photo, this loving, silly picture of their kiss before the race.

They checked their water bottles and joined the host of runners talking, eating, stretching, and jogging in place.

"Just pray that I finish." She didn't handle the longer distance as well as Jason. She tugged on his arm. "Let's move toward the back. I'd rather not get squished at our first Blueberry Stomp."

The starter raised his gun, and the crowd grew quiet.

"Ready. Set."

Bang!

Callie and Jason moved as part of an enormous, energetic blob that flowed down Michigan Street. She concentrated so hard on staying beside her husband in the crush that she hardly noticed the people lining the streets.

After the runners left the city limits, they spread out. Callie ran easily beside Jason on this gorgeous September morning. As they ran along Eleventh Road, he checked their time, as always. She checked out the shady forests, green fields blanketed with goldenrod, and the blue morning glories spiraled up corn stalks. On Nutmeg Road, they passed the site where Andrea and Patrick were building their spacious new house. Callie didn't feel the least bit envious. She and Jason had found a modest fix-it-up 1930s bungalow on South Michigan they both loved.

She grinned at her husband. Though running, he managed to tickle the back of her neck. They'd probably work together on their house—and their differing attitudes toward money!—a long time. But both projects would prove worth it.

They made frequent water stops and paced themselves. Callie began to feel that she really could do this. Even her veil stayed on.

"You okay?" Jason asked several times.

"'m good." She really was.

til they reentered the city limits. By now, they'd slowed,

so she began to notice spectators clapping for them and yelling congratulations. Jason tipped his hat to several.

Oh yes. The veil. She tried to look the part of a smiling, blushing bride, but mostly just tried to breathe.

"You can do it, Callie." Jason's smile kept her going. "We're almost there."

They were entering downtown. *Help, Lord. I want to do this with Jason.*

Less than a mile from the finish…

The crowd clapped and hurrahed. She waved at Pastor Sam and his family. At more friends from Eastside. Dr. Tom and Dr. Linda popped up from lawn chairs across from Treat's to cheer them on.

"You're doing great, Callie. We're almost to The Place."

Jason remembered. She wanted to throw herself down on the spot and laugh.

The Taylor clan had set up there again. As one, they boinged like a herd of Tiggers.

"Yay, Callie! Yay, Jason!"

"*Woo-hoo* for Mr. and Mrs. Kenton!" Andrea whooped at the top of her lungs. "Yay, Callie. You go, girl!"

This time, I'm staying on my feet. Callie threw a kiss to them, new energy flowing into her weary muscles. Lifting her head and fists, she plowed past The Place, waving to all who applauded. Soon she saw Aunt Sheila and Uncle Alan. They stood in the KFC parking lot, waving drumsticks at them.

The sight that nearly made her fall to her knees was Brandy, waiting at the finish line. Clapping. She was clapping as Callie and Jason, holding hands, approached. Looking Callie straight in the eye, Brandy opened her arms.

Callie ran into them. Jason joined her in the hug.

She wasn't Miss Blueberry anymore. But that was just fine with her.

* * * * *

REQUEST YOUR FREE BOOKS!

2 FREE CHRISTIAN NOVELS
PLUS 2
FREE
MYSTERY GIFTS

HEARTSONG PRESENTS

YES! Please send me 2 Free Heartsong Presents novels and my 2 FREE mystery gifts (gifts are worth about $10). After receiving them, if I don't wish to receive any more books I can return the shipping statement marked "cancel." If I don't cancel, I will receive 4 brand-new novels every month and be billed just $4.24 per book. That's a savings of 20% off the cover price. It's quite a bargain! Shipping and handling is just 50¢ per book in the U.S.* I understand that accepting the 2 free books and gifts places me under no obligation to buy anything. I can always return a shipment and cancel at any time. Even if I never buy another book, the two free books and gifts are mine to keep forever.

159 HDN FT97

Name _____ (PLEASE PRINT)

Address _____ Apt. #

City _____ State _____ Zip _____

Signature (if under 18, a parent or guardian must sign)

Mail to the **Reader Service:**
IN U.S.A.: P.O. Box 1867, Buffalo, NY 14240-1867

Not valid for current subscribers to Heartsong Presents books.

* Terms and prices subject to change without notice. Prices do not include applicable taxes. Sales tax applicable in N.Y. This offer is limited to one order per household. All orders subject to credit approval. Credit or debit balances in a customer's account(s) may be offset by any other outstanding balance owed by or to the customer. Please allow 4 to 6 weeks for delivery. Offer available while quantities last. Offer valid only in the U.S.

Your Privacy—The Reader Service is committed to protecting your privacy. Our Privacy Policy is available online at www.ReaderService.com or upon request from the Reader Service.

We make a portion of our mailing list available to reputable third parties that offer products we believe may interest you. If you prefer that we not exchange your name with third parties, or if you wish to clarify or modify your communication preferences, please visit us at www.ReaderService.com/consumerschoice or write to us at Reader Service Preference Service, P.O. Box 9062, Buffalo, NY 14269. Include your complete name and address.

HSP12